TUNNELS
of TREACHERY

TUNNELS *of* TREACHERY

ANOTHER MOOSE JAW ADVENTURE

MARY HARELKIN BISHOP

COTEAU BOOKS
WWW.COTEAUBOOKS.COM

Edited by Barbara Sapergia.
Cover illustration by Dawn Pearcey.
Cover and book design by Duncan Campbell.
Printed and bound in Canada at Transcontinental Printing.

National Library of Canada Cataloguing in Publication Data

Bishop, Mary Harelkin, 1958-
Tunnels of treachery : another Moose Jaw adventure / Mary Harelkin Bishop.

ISBN 1-55050-270-0

I. Title.
PS8553.I849T87 2003   jC813'.6   C2003-911241-1

10 9 8 7 6 5 4 3 2 1

COTEAU BOOKS
401-2206 Dewdney Ave
Regina, Saskatchewan
Canada S4R 1H3

available in Canada and the US from:
Fitzhenry & Whiteside
195 Allstate Parkway
Markham, Ontario
Canada L3R 4T8

The publisher gratefully acknowledges the financial assistance of the Saskatchewan Arts Board, the Canada Council for the Arts, the Government of Canada through the Book Publishing Industry Development Program (BPIDP), and the City of Regina Arts Commission, for its publishing program.

TABLE *of* CONTENTS

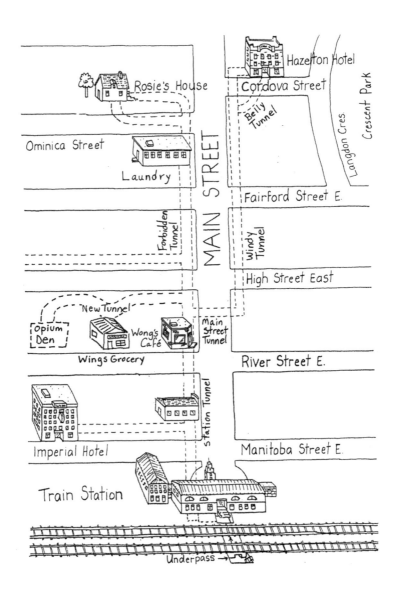

ABOVE GROUND

To my nieces and nephews,
Jared, Isaac, Kelsey, and Holly,
with love.

STORIES?! WHO WANTS STORIES?

"Tell stories about the old days, Grandpa," Andrea begged as thunder shook the house again.

A bolt of lightning seemed to come right through the large picture window, giving the crowded living room an eerie glow. When the storm had finally hit the dusty streets of Moose Jaw a few minutes ago, the large party had moved indoors. Most of the guests now gathered in the crowded living room, some spilling out into the narrow hallway and into the kitchen; damp, rain-speckled bodies pressed together as laughter and merriment filled the air.

Andrea had managed to squeeze her way into the living room and now sat at her grandparents' feet, looking up into their glowing faces. It wasn't everyday that her whole family gathered for a celebration, and she knew how happy her grandparents were. It was their 70th wedding anniversary.

Every member of the Talbot family and extended family had come for the anniversary, each bringing a story or memento to share, since her grandparents had insisted that there be no gifts. "Your presence is your gift," Grandma Talbot kept saying; so the family had decided to go one step further and dress for the occasion, in costumes representing earlier periods of Moose Jaw history.

Andrea had chosen to wear her oldest jean overalls and an ancient blue flannel work shirt that belonged to her father. She also wore a soft-brimmed cap like the one Vance had lent her during her first tunnel adventure. "I'm a tunnel runner," she proudly told anyone who asked her. "You know, like the boys who used to do errands and lead people in the tunnels back in the 1920s."

Her relatives had smiled indulgently, remembering that she had also been wearing the overalls the night of her cousin Vanessa's wedding rehearsal a few summers ago. They were all used to Andrea's antics, for she didn't look or act her age. At fifteen, most girls would be more interested in dressing up in fancy clothes, but not Andrea. She preferred the tomboy look.

Ten-year-old Tony had decided to dress in the same period costume. He wore dark trousers rolled up to just below his knees, held up by a pair of suspenders and a white dress shirt. On his head was a cap similar to Andrea's.

Lightning flashed again and a huge crash of thunder sent kids and pets scurrying for cover. "Maybe we'll get lucky and get to go back in time again," Tony whispered to Andrea, looking very hopeful. His knapsack was packed with all his medical supplies and some snacks, and sat ready and waiting in Grandpa's office in the basement. If they were going back in time again, he wanted to be prepared. The idea of ending up in the past without his insulin did not appeal to him in the least.

"It looks like we may be sitting in the dark soon," Grandma Talbot said, watching out the window as the wind whipped through the branches of a tall poplar tree in the yard.

"What will we do then?" Tony scooted closer to Andrea as thunder echoed in the distance. He hated storms, although he'd never admit it.

"Do tell stories, Vance," Grandma encouraged, shifting around to get comfortable beside him on the overstuffed couch. "Remember when our children were young, before we got a television? You told the best stories."

"Tell about how you two first discovered you were falling in love!" Aunt Bea threw in. She was sitting in the comfortable armchair nearby. "I love that story."

"Yes, tell stories about the tunnels!" Tony begged with excitement. "Tell about Moose Jaw, when you were growing up, Grandpa."

"Sh-h-h," Andrea warned, poking Tony in the ribs with her elbow. She didn't want him giving away her secret, and she was afraid that, in his excitement, Tony would forget and blab it to everyone. After all, she had managed to keep her time travel adventure back to the 1920s of Moose Jaw a secret for a whole year.

It would still have been a secret, but Tony had read her diary last year, telling how she had gone back in time and met gangsters and become a tunnel runner. She had been so furious with him that she'd left the house, leaving him all alone. When she'd returned several minutes later, the old wooden cupboard in the basement, which stood in front of a tunnel entrance, was open and Tony had disappeared. Figuring that Tony had gone into the tunnels, Andrea had had no choice but to follow him. They'd both ended up back in the past and together had a dangerous time with Moose Jaw's corrupt police force. They had also met Great Aunt Bea and Grandpa Talbot as kids of twelve and fifteen.

They certainly had stories they could share, Andrea thought, a teasing smile on her lips. But who would believe them?

"Tell us about the tunnels," Tony repeated, moving away from Andrea's sharp elbow.

"There are many stories that need to be told," Grandpa Talbot agreed, glancing beside him on the couch to where Mr. and Mrs. Mark sat. The two couples had been good friends for many years, their children growing up together and becoming friends as well. And now their grandchildren were friends too.

The Marks looked cute sitting together, wrinkles defining facial features, hair mostly white now. Mrs. Mark was small and frail, stooped with age and slow moving, but her mind was sharp. Her face was always calm and serene, but marked by scars that were now almost lost in the wrinkles of her cheeks. The scars ran down her right cheek, over her neck and down her arm. Andrea had always wondered about them, but had never been brave enough to ask.

Mr. Mark now walked with a cane and his clothes hung loosely on his body, giving him a frail appearance. But he usually had a twinkle in his eyes and a baritone laugh that was contagious. They hadn't always been old, Andrea realized. Once they had been young and energetic, and she wondered what stories of their youth they could tell.

"You have many tales to tell too, old friend," Grandpa Talbot said, patting Mr. Mark's bony shoulder and then squeezing his forearm. "Perhaps now is the time to share them."

Mr. Mark sat silent for so long that Andrea was sure he hadn't heard. She wondered if he was getting hard of hearing. Finally he began to speak, slowly and deliberately, as if he had to think about which words he wanted to say. His accent was strong, making it difficult to understand him at times. It just made Andrea listen more closely; she didn't want to miss any of the stories he was about to tell.

"I have many secrets," he agreed, a note of sadness in his words. "But what good is sharing the past? It is gone and no one can change it. There were many difficult times, Vance." He sat absently rubbing his left forearm. "Perhaps it is best to let sleeping dogs lie."

"What does that mean?" Tony asked, confused by the strange figure of speech.

"It means Mr. Mark thinks we should leave the past in the past and not bother about it," Aunt Bea replied.

"Tell your stories," Grandma encouraged. "Your family, your grandchildren, need to hear them, just as ours need to hear our stories, and yours as well. The hard times, the pain and sorrow, the joys, this is the glue that holds families together. The stories are a thread, woven through the fabric of life, connecting all of us, not just families, but friends as well."

She smiled at her dearest friends. "You know as well as I that our families are connected. We have shared many times, good and bad, and because of them, we have become good friends; as close to family as you can get without actually being related. What would Vance and I have done without you two in our lives?"

Mr. Mark studied the people waiting patiently for the stories to begin. They sat two and three on the couches and chairs and then spread out on the carpet in front of them. "Your grandchildren are most eager to hear the stories," he pointed out, looking at Andrea and Tony and all the others sitting expectantly at their feet. A sad smile made his lips quiver. "My grandchildren are nowhere to be seen. They don't want to hear about the old ways. They only want to be Canadian."

"But they are Canadian!" Tony piped up, his blue eyes puzzled. "They were born right here in Moose Jaw."

Mrs. Mark shook her head slowly. "They do not think they look Canadian."

"What does a Canadian look like?" Tony asked, even more confused.

Mr. Mark laughed. "Why, just like you, young Tony, at least that's what they think. They want to be blonde with blue eyes. They are ashamed to be Chinese and to have grandparents who speak English with such funny accents."

"They refuse to speak Chinese," Mrs. Mark added, "even though they have known it since they were babies. They are not eager to work at the restaurant because their friends might see them and tease them." She looked sadly about the room. "Our grandchildren do not want to learn the family history. They don't want to hear the stories."

"You could start with the exciting stories," Tony offered. "You could talk about the tunnels!" He was taking every opportunity to bring up the subject. "I'll bet you even have tunnels in your restaurant!" A look of alarm darted across Mr. Mark's face so quickly that Andrea almost missed it. He did know something about the tunnels, she was sure of that.

"Be quiet, Tony," Grandpa Talbot quickly ordered. "Let the Marks decide for themselves which stories they want to share."

Andrea felt sad for the Marks. She knew how hard they had worked to make their restaurant a great success. It was one of the busiest and most popular restaurants in Moose Jaw, proudly standing in a brick building right on Main Street, and they were proud of it. She knew what a wonderful family they had. She had known the Mark grandchildren, Eddie and Kami, forever. They got together almost every time the Talbot family came to Moose Jaw. Still, there was a lot she didn't know about them, she realized.

"Where are Kami and Eddie?" Andrea whispered to Tony, her eyes searching the crowded room. "They should be here listening to their grandparents tell stories. They might learn something."

Ignoring the feeling that she should leave well enough alone and not meddle in other people's business, Andrea whispered, "Come on, Tony, I'm going to find Kami and Eddie."

"They're probably downstairs in Grandpa's office playing computer games," Tony said, reluctantly rising to his feet and following along. "They won't want to be dragged upstairs to listen to stories."

"You're right," Andrea agreed, slowly weaving her way through the guests on the floor and out into the hallway. "But they need to be here. I feel so sad for the Marks. Can you imagine being embarrassed because of our grandparents?"

"No way!" Tony shook his head so emphatically he almost lost his cap. "Grandpa Vance is so cool! And I like Grandma, too, and Aunt Bea!"

"Maybe we just like them so much because we went back in time and met them when they were young. Maybe if we only knew them as old people we wouldn't like them as much," Andrea said as she headed down the basement stairs toward the office, her brown eyes thoughtful.

"Maybe," Tony replied, "but I don't think so. I liked Aunt Bea and Grandpa Vance a lot even before I traveled back in time last year. Now that I know them as kids, I just like them better, that's all."

Thunder rumbled overhead and the huge house trembled. "I don't like this storm." Andrea grabbed onto the banister for support as she descended the stairs. Her fingers tingled and the tiny hairs on the back of her neck stood up. She had the strangest feeling of déjà vu.

"It's scary, even though we're all together in the house. It feels as if there's an energy field or an electrical force running through the house." She rubbed her arms to get rid of the goosebumps. "Can you feel it?"

"No." Sniffing, his nose in the air, Tony shook his head. "It just feels like a storm. It smells like rain."

They had reached the bottom of the stairs. Andrea shivered, hugging her arms close to her body. "I feel cold and hot and clammy at the same time. It feels like —" Abruptly, she clamped her lips together, keeping the words trapped inside. She didn't want Tony to know that the last time she'd felt like this they had ended up in the past.

Tony turned the knob and pushed the door wide open. "See, I told you," he said, catching a glimpse of the twins at the computer. They sat at Grandpa Talbot's wooden desk, their noses almost pressed against the large computer screen. Loud and annoying music filled the room.

"They're playing computer games. How are we going to drag them away from all this fun and excitement?" Tony rolled his eyes when Andrea threw him a questioning look. "I'm being sarcastic, you know," he told her. "Don't they know real people are more important than games and machines?"

Andrea headed toward the twins. "If worst comes to worst," she grinned menacingly over her shoulder at Tony, wiggling her eyebrows up and down, "we'll just pull the plug!

"Hey, you two need to get upstairs right away," Andrea said firmly, her hands on her hips.

The twins didn't take their eyes from the screen. "Says who?" Kami asked, absently, her eyes glued to the screen.

"Yeah," Eddie echoed. At fourteen, he and his sister were just developing the adolescent, "I could care less" attitude about life.

"Your grandparents, that's who." Leaning over the desk Andrea blocked their view, finally managing to get their attention.

With a sigh of impatience, Kami brushed gleaming black bangs from her face. Her long hair was braided in one thick braid and hung down her back, stark against the crisp white costume she wore. Dark almond-shaped eyes snapped in irritation. "I don't want to sit there listening to a bunch of old geezers tell dumb stories," she announced, trying to push Andrea out of the way.

"They're not old geezers," Tony defended them. "Your grandparents are as nice as ours. I don't know why you don't like them."

"Oh, they're all right, I suppose," Eddie conceded. "But who wants to listen to a bunch of garbage about the good old days?"

That sounded harsh, even to Kami, and she tried

to soften his words. "It's just that they always want to talk about how things used to be. They made us come to this anniversary party and they made us dress up! Look at me!" Kami wailed, holding up her arms for inspection.

Pressing her lips together to keep from smiling, Andrea studied the twins. They wore traditional Chinese outfits she had seen in old photographs. Long white tunics made of heavy cloth fell almost to their knees. White trousers of the same material hung long and baggy beneath the tunics. Two small round caps lay scrunched up on the desk beside the computer monitor.

"Can you believe they used to wear this stuff?" Kami sniffed, looking down at the offending outfit.

Eddie sighed. "It's so stupid. And they want us to speak Chinese too." He trailed off. "Why speak Chinese when nobody will understand us?"

"You don't know what it's like," Kami muttered, her thumbs clicking on the buttons of the computer game. "You don't look different and have grandparents who talk funny."

Why, they're jealous of us, Andrea realized, feeling something begin to prick at her conscience. Maybe that was why the twins sometimes acted strange. Maybe they missed being with their parents too; they always seemed to be off to various parts of the world pursuing their own careers.

"Come on, you two," Andrea coaxed, trying to sound reasonable. "It's really not that bad upstairs."

"No way," Eddie's words were short and to the point, and Andrea suddenly realized how stubborn he could be.

"Please," she pleaded, wracking her brain to come up with something enticing to draw them upstairs.

"They're telling stories about the tunnels," Tony persuaded, his voice inviting. "I'll bet your grandparents have lots of stories to tell about adventures in the tunnels."

"We don't believe in the tunnels," Kami stated, folding her arms over her chest. "It's all just a plot to get tourists to spend time and money in little old Moose Jaw."

"It isn't either," Tony replied, getting hot beneath the collar.

"It's all a hoax," Eddie supplied, tapping Tony on the arm with his cap.

"B-but," Andrea sputtered, "there are tunnels right in your grandparents' restaurant!"

Kami didn't take her eyes off the screen, her fingers moving busily on the controls. "That's just the basement – it was built like...like a maze, short and narrow, with lots of hiding places."

Andrea was flabbergasted. Maybe Kami knew more than she let on. She wished she had been allowed into that basement just once to have a look for herself.

The storm seemed to intensify. Lightning flashed several times in a row, so brightly that it reflected into the basement windows. Loud crashes of thunder reverberated through the air as the lights flickered again. The computer screen blinked. "You'd better shut down the computer," Andrea advised, listening as the wind howled around the house. It rattled the windows, and she felt the hairs stand up on the back of her neck again. "If the power goes off suddenly, the computer might get damaged."

"We're going to finish our game first," Kami flung the words over her shoulder. "We'll come upstairs when we're good and ready!"

Andrea watched helplessly as the twins continued to play. She shrugged her shoulders at Tony. "Now what do we do?"

As if on cue, the two grandmothers popped their snowy heads into the room. "Oh," Grandma Talbot said from the doorway, "I see Andrea and Tony have already invited you to come upstairs for the stories. Hurry, you don't want to miss any of them."

"We're just going to play computer games," Kami said, her back to the door. "We don't want to hear stories."

"Kami and Eddie, your grandfather and I would really like you to come and listen. To stay down here in the basement is to be rude to him and to our hosts. There are many stories you need to hear about your heritage. They are important. Now put your caps on

14

and come upstairs now."

Silently the twins looked at one another and then pulled the round caps on. "There," Eddie said, going back to his game. "But you can't make us go upstairs."

Mrs. Mark shrugged, not wanting to fight with her grandchildren in public. Andrea could see hurt and disappointment wash over her face, the scars on her neck turning red from embarrassment. Andrea wished she could do something to help get the twins upstairs.

"Someday, you will realize how important the stories are," Mrs. Mark admonished, wagging a bony finger at their backs. "Remember my words, Kami and Eddie. You will live to regret this foolish selfishness of yours. One way or another, you will learn the stories..." And with those stern words, she walked out and shut the door, leaving Andrea pondering their meaning.

Tony lost his patience with the twins. "That's it," he yelled, pushing his way between the computer desk and the wall to get at the electrical outlet. "I'm unplugging this stupid computer!"

"No!" Kami bellowed. "Just let me finish this level and save it!" She grabbed Tony's arm and tried to push him away.

Fending her off with one hand, Tony stretched his other arm out, reaching for the plug. "It's just a silly game!"

"Help, Eddie!" Kami called.

Eddie raced to her rescue. "Get away from there!" He pulled at Tony's waist, trying to drag him away from the wall. The three of them tussled and tugged like puppies straining for a juicy bone.

"Cut it out, you guys," Andrea yelled. "I can't believe it; all this fuss for a stupid computer game!"

An enormous crash of thunder boomed. Lightning flashed as the lights flickered and went out, leaving the four in almost total darkness in the basement room. An eerie glow seemed to come from the large old cupboard in the corner of the room. A loud humming noise filled the room and the armoire began to swing open, revealing a huge hole in the wall.

Tony triumphantly waved the plug in the air. "I did it!" He staggered backward, trying to free himself and pitched heavily into Kami and Eddie, knocking them off balance. They teetered and tipped, arms flailing, and tumbled into the black void behind the armoire.

INTO THE TUNNELS

Staring into the dark space where the twins had just disappeared, Andrea moaned and sank to the floor in shock, her body trembling. "Oh no!" she wailed. "You pushed the twins into the tunnel!"

"I didn't push them!" Tony said excitedly. Now he and Andrea would have to go after them. He didn't really care why they had to go back, he was just glad it had happened. He grinned, trotting across the room to grab his backpack. "We're going back in time!"

"I'm not going after them, and you're not either! Let them stay in the tunnels, for all I care! They don't even believe in them! Well, now they'll know better."

Andrea knew she was talking nonsense, but the last thing she wanted to do was go back into the tunnels for a third time. What if someone got hurt, or even killed?

"Don't be silly," Tony cried, grabbing at her arm. "We have to rescue them, Andrea! The armoire is still moved away from the wall. It's waiting for us!"

Andrea stared at the gaping hole. "This is all your fault!" she shouted, turning her fear and anger on Tony. "They could be in big trouble down there!"

Shuddering, Tony suddenly remembered the peril they had all been in the year before. "Come on, Andrea. We have to go get them. They're probably scared out of their minds! They might be in danger! Let's go get them."

Andrea hesitated. She was more frightened of going back to the past this time than she had been before. But Tony was right. They couldn't just leave the twins in the tunnels. She took a step closer to the armoire, her foot catching on something. Glancing down she saw the electrical cord wrapped around her ankle. She tried to shake the cord loose, but lost her balance and began to fall. Tony grabbed her arm to steady her and they both fell into the blackness behind the armoire.

Looking back toward the safety of the basement room, Andrea saw the armoire begin to swing shut. An invisible force grabbed at her body as tentacles of time pulled her along at super speeds. Bright lights flashed and her body began to tingle and vibrate, as if every hair was electrified and hypersensitive. She was certain her blonde straw hair would have stood on end had it not been safely tucked up under the cap.

Slowly, the world stopped spinning and Andrea found herself standing in a narrow tunnel clutching Tony's hand.

"We made it!" Tony pulled his hand from Andrea's vise grip and pumped a fist in the air in celebration. "We've gone back in time!"

Andrea carefully studied their surroundings. "Something's not right."

The only light seemed to be coming from the disappearing, softly glowing time warp behind them. She looked along the tunnel in front of them, fighting that familiar feeling of claustrophobia. The walls of the tunnel seemed to close in on her in the vanishing light as the darkness played tricks with her mind. She realized that they were in one of the short tunnels that led to Rosie's house.

"But something's different," she whispered to herself as she studied the walls. In the gathering darkness she caught sight of a lantern hanging nearby. "It's not lit! The lantern's not lit! Something is wrong."

"Get the flashlight," Tony said, turning his back to Andrea. He heard the rasp of the zipper as she opened the backpack and rummaged around inside.

"Here it is." Andrea clicked the button and a stream of bright light filled the tunnel. "Let's go slowly," she said, pushing Tony behind her. "I have a bad feeling about this."

They clung to one another, creeping along as sounds of small scurrying feet came from above. Shuddering, Andrea ducked her head, pulling her neck into her shoulders. "I think I hear mice or rats up there." She glanced toward the ceiling, then pulled the cap low over her eyes.

"Don't think about it," Tony said quickly, grabbing her wrist and pulling her along. "Keep walking."

The journey seemed endless, but Andrea knew the distance they actually covered was short. It was only a matter of twenty metres or so before they would reach the small junction in the tunnel. She knew that if they then turned left, they would be in the tunnel that led to the cellar entrance at Rosie's house. If they turned right, they would be heading toward the storage area.

They passed another lantern hanging lifeless and cold on a wooden post. "Why aren't the lanterns lit?" Andrea wondered aloud. "I don't like this."

"Which way shall we look first?" Tony asked, excitement making his voice high. "I think we should go to Grandpa's – I mean Rosie's – place, and say hi. I can't wait to see everyone again!"

Andrea wished he would just be quiet for a minute to let her think. Everything felt wrong this time, and Tony just couldn't feel the danger the way she could; it was like a sixth sense. All he was thinking about was having a good time with Vance and Beanie. He didn't realize how serious this could be.

The light from the flashlight bounced off a dark wooden surface just ahead of them. "What's that up there?" Tony asked.

"It looks like the tunnel is boarded up," Andrea replied, anxiety beginning to gnaw at her stomach. Worried and scared, she tried not to let the emotions show, not wanting to upset Tony.

Cautiously they moved closer, the light reflecting on pieces of knotted wood. Planks were nailed across the tunnel. It was blocked.

"So that's why the lanterns aren't lit down here; this entrance is sealed," Tony surmised.

Andrea knew she had to find Kami and Eddie, so she might as well make the best of it. Maybe, if she planned it right, she and Tony would find them very quickly and they would be back to the present before bedtime.

"Where can the twins be?" She ran the beam of light around the edges of the boards. A small hole appeared at the bottom near the ground. Two boards had been pried loose and left to hang lop-sided toward the ground.

"I'll bet they crawled through there," Tony said, bending down to inspect the hole. "Look at this." He came back up, a small piece of heavy white cloth pinched between his thumb and finger.

"It came from one of their costumes," Andrea decided, studying the tiny piece of fabric Tony had placed in the palm of her hand. "It looks like they crawled through." Pocketing the piece of material, she got down on all fours. "Help me pry another board loose, Tony. I'm too big to get through that narrow hole."

Together they pulled at the board. A long screeching sound pierced the silence as the nails pulled loose. "Sh-h-h," Andrea cautioned.

"I know," Tony whispered.

Andrea got down on her stomach and slid through the small opening. Tony passed his backpack through and then squirmed after her. Jumping to his feet, he shouldered his backpack, looking around. "Now things look okay," he said with satisfaction as weak light blinked from a lantern hanging to their right way down the tunnel. It lit the way south toward the storage area.

"I don't know," Andrea said uncertainly, aiming the flashlight to her left, down the tunnel toward the cellar entrance to Rosie's place. "Why aren't those lanterns lit?" she asked, staring into the black void.

Turning left, they walked together in the black tunnel, the light from the flashlight bouncing on the dirt and gravel of the tunnel floor.

"This looks the same," Tony said. "This part always looks like a dead-end, remember?"

Andrea did remember, but she didn't feel confident about it. They reached the area where the door should have been. In its place they found more wooden boards. They stretched from floor to ceiling, totally blocking this passageway to Rosie's house as well. "I wonder what's going on?" she asked again, carefully shining the light around the edges of the boards. This time there were no loose boards to pry up.

"Maybe I can pull one loose." Tony gritted his teeth as he attacked the boards. Nothing moved. "Why have they boarded up these tunnels?" He sank down on his knees in the gravel, owl eyes of fear looking back at Andrea.

"Remember our time-travel trip last year?" Tony said. " Didn't Officer Paterson say that he would clean up the tunnels? Maybe this was his way of keeping people out."

"It's not keeping everyone out," Andrea whispered. The hairs on the back of her neck stood up in fear as she turned around and stared at a lantern hanging way down the tunnel. It sputtered weakly, a guiding light to anyone heading toward the storage area.

"Someone's using the tunnels again, and I bet they're up to no good," Tony breathed.

They both stood frozen in place as frightening memories besieged them.

"We're wasting our time here," Andrea finally spoke, pushing the memories away. Turning south, she grabbed Tony's hand and headed toward the storage area.

"We have to find Kami and Eddie and get out of here. Let's go to the storage area. You do remember how the tunnels work, don't you?" Andrea asked. "Let me show you, just in case we get separated down here."

"Separated?" Tony became glued to Andrea's side, both hands clutching her wrist. "I won't let us get separated."

"Well, just in case." Andrea bent down, and using a small stick she had found lying in the dirt, she mapped out the tunnels as she remembered them. "We're in the tunnel that goes north to Rosie's place; you know, the one that leads to the cellar entrance. Only it's sealed up. If we turn back, we'll pass the blocked entrance we crawled through. If we keep going south, we'll end up in the underground storage area."

She drew a rectangle representing the large cavern. "The storage area is connected to the warehouse by the wooden door here," she said, marking a spot in the centre of the west wall of the rectangle. On the south side, she drew in the Forbidden tunnel.

"Remember, the Forbidden tunnel is the narrow and really dark one. It connects to the tunnel that leads to the train station. The Main Street tunnel runs east under Main Street to the Windy tunnel, which leads to the Hazelton Hotel."

"I remember," Tony said grimly. "Let's go find Kami and Eddie."

"Sh-h-h," Andrea warned, stepping in front of Tony. "Remember, we need to be quiet down here. Sounds travel very far through these tunnels, and we don't want to be found out." As they neared the storage area she quickly switched off the flashlight hoping that no one had seen the light bouncing as they walked.

Poking her head around the corner of the tunnel, Andrea listened. Her ears strained as her eyes slowly adjusted to the light from a few lanterns hanging in the underground cavern. It was amazing how fast she readapted to life as a tunnel runner. Feeling like a crafty nocturnal creature, she crept silently along the wall.

"I hear some very strange noises coming from over there," she whispered. "I'll go first, but you stay close behind. I don't want to lose you too!"

Together, they moved into the storage area, Tony clutching the back of Andrea's overalls. Gravel slipped under their feet and she held her breath, hoping the soft scuffing sounds they were making wouldn't attract anyone's attention.

Noises sounded again from the far corner of the storage area and Andrea froze in her tracks. Tony couldn't see and collided with her, his nose bumping between her shoulder blades. "Ouch," he muttered, taking a step back.

Andrea could hear the friction of skin on skin as he rubbed his nose. "Sh-h-h," she whispered impatiently. "It sounds like someone is moving something heavy, like a box." She strained her ears until the silence thrummed in her eardrums, drowning out the other noises.

Clutching Tony's hand, she moved toward the sound. Slowly shapes began to appear. Andrea could make out several rough wooden tables lined up against the dirt wall on both sides of the door to the warehouse. Broken wooden cases had been tossed about and pieces of wood of all shapes and sizes lay about the area, making movement difficult.

Shuddering, Andrea recalled her terrible ordeal in that warehouse and it took every ounce of courage she had not to flee back up the tunnel. She had been dragged through that very door and then tied up in an office while the men tried to decide what to do with her. The thought of being kidnapped again caused a slow dance of anxiety in her stomach. Forcibly she pushed it down, reminding herself that all the bad guys had been arrested.

A sound, almost like a sob, seemed to come from under the tables. Certain that it was some sort of animal, Andrea prepared to run. It happened again, half hiccup, half sob that was definitely human. "Stay here," she ordered. Moving quietly, she approached the tables and then dropped to her knees to peer underneath. "Kami!"

Disheveled, tears streaming down her face, Kami crawled out from under the table and threw her arms around Andrea, sobbing loudly. "Sh-h-h," Andrea warned, awkwardly patting her back. "It's not that bad. You'll get used to the dark down here."

"Wh-where are we?" Kami asked, her words barely audible through her sobs.

"It's okay, Kami," Andrea said, smoothing her friend's bangs away from her face. "You're safe," she soothed, although her stomach clenched at the words.

"I don't think we're very safe here," Tony pointed out, looking in the direction of the wooden door. It was so close he could have reached out and touched it. "Someone could come rushing out of that door and we'd all be caught!"

"Caught?" Kami choked. "What do you mean?"

Suddenly faint voices came from behind the door and Andrea froze, her breath catching in her throat. There was nowhere to run and hide. The voices faded and she breathed again. "We'd better get out of here."

"But we need to look for Eddie, first," Tony reminded her.

Andrea nodded. "I'll go look in the Forbidden tunnel, just in case he's there. You stay here with Kami. Is that okay with you, Kami?"

"Find Eddie fast and let's get out of here. I hate this place," Kami sobbed.

"You go quickly and come right back," Tony said, patting Kami's arm in comfort. "I hate being left in the dark. Down here anything could happen..."

MEET MEAN-EYED MAX

Andrea inched her way through the Forbidden tunnel, every nerve in her body at high alert to sense danger. Even the hair on her head felt as if it was standing at attention. The light from the flashlight seemed to get swallowed up by the blackness, and Andrea felt the tunnel walls began to close in on her. She hated the Forbidden tunnel more than any of the others, and for good reason too. Her old nightmares centred around it.

Muted noises from behind her kicked her heart into overdrive and Andrea felt her head begin to whirl. Don't faint, she ordered sternly. That would be the stupidest thing she could do. The noises tapered off and Andrea was sure that her over-sensitized ears had just imagined it. Then a loud scream reverberated through the Forbidden tunnel, becoming more intense as it bounced back and forth between the narrow walls.

"Kami!" Andrea cried, recognizing the voice. Whirling around, she raced back the way she had come.

The flashlight beam bounced off the tunnel walls as she ran, causing a strobe-light effect, which made her dizzy. The tunnel was suffocating and endless. It reminded her of her nightmares from last year. She hadn't thought about them for a long time now. Was she doomed to spend the rest of her life running endlessly through this horrible tunnel?

Suddenly the entrance to the storage area loomed ahead. Skidding to a halt Andrea flicked off the light and moved cautiously against the wall. The thundering of her heart and her gasping breath made hearing difficult and she willed herself to calm down. Inhaling deep breaths through her nose, she exhaled slowly through parched lips and her heartbeat slowed a bit.

Andrea heard quiet sobs as she slipped into the storage area. It appeared to be empty. Who had made all of that noise? The sobs sounded like... "Tony?" Andrea whispered into the dark. "Is that you?"

A small body launched itself into her arms, almost knocking her off her feet. "I lost her," he sobbed, burying his face in the bib of her overalls. "I lost her. Some mean-looking men came and grabbed her. They came through the door. They took her away and gave me these when I tried to rescue her!" Tony held out a trembling hand.

"What is it?" Andrea said, still trying to piece together his disjointed story. Holding his palm up for closer inspection, she flicked the flashlight on. Five coins winked at her.

"They paid me for her," Tony cried, fresh tears rolling down his cheeks. "But they said they never wanted to see me in the tunnels again."

"They paid you?" Andrea shook her head, totally bewildered. "That doesn't make any sense."

"They said I'd found something they'd lost. They dragged her away through the door, Andrea." He turned and pointed at the warehouse door, now firmly shut. "What are we going to do?"

Utterly confused, Andrea gave Tony a brief hug. "It's okay, Tony. You couldn't have stopped them. We'll find her, don't worry." But anxiety gnawed at her churning stomach.

What did those men want with Kami? Something didn't add up, but Andrea couldn't figure out what it was. All she wanted to do was get back to the present as soon as possible, and now they were back to square one. "Well, come on, then, let's go see if we can find Eddie. I only got about halfway through the Forbidden tunnel when I heard Kami scream."

She studied the heavy wooden door, a sinking feeling spreading in the pit of her stomach. "I think they might have grabbed Kami because they think she belongs here."

"What do you mean?" Tony turned huge eyes toward Andrea.

"I think they paid you for her because they thought you brought them an illegal immigrant!"

"What?" Tony was completely baffled.

Remembering what she knew about the history of the Chinese people in Canada, Andrea explained, "I think Kami has been mistaken for one of the indentured servants brought over from China to work in Canada in the early 1900s."

"You think Kami is going to have to work in one of those awful laundries or something, like a slave?" Tony's voice trembled, his eyes filling with tears.

"Not a slave, exactly," Andrea gently corrected. She could see how upset Tony was getting. "They were indentured servants. I did a Heritage Project for school last year on the building of the railway in Canada and I learned a lot about the Chinese people and why they came to Canada."

"Why did they come?" Tony asked. "Were they captured like the African people in the United States and brought over as slaves?"

"It wasn't quite like that in Canada," Andrea explained. "The Chinese men were brought over to help build the railway. They were given the most dangerous jobs and paid half what the Eurpoeans got paid."

"Half!" Tony sounded shocked. "But that's not fair!"

"And that's not all," Andrea continued. "When they wanted to stay in Canada, the government introduced the Head Tax and the Chinese people had to pay it before they could stay in Canada legally."

Tony thought about that for a moment. "I'll bet it took a long time to save up money to pay that tax."

"It took years," Andrea agreed. "Some people think the Chinese immigrants worked and lived in the tunnels while they saved money to pay the Head Tax. Some bad guys used the people as servants and made them work hard for poor wages doing really terrible jobs."

"You think that's what happened with Kami, don't you?" Tony whispered, his fingers cold and clammy on her arm.

Nodding, Andrea squeezed his hands in hers. "This problem is too big for us to handle alone. We need help."

"Let's go find Vance and Beanie first," Tony agreed, looking longingly toward the tunnel that should have led to Rosie's house. "They'll help us."

"I was thinking of Officer Paterson," Andrea said, turning briskly toward the Forbidden tunnel. "Let's just find a way out of here and get his help." She shone the flashlight at their feet as they moved away from the door. "What's this?" A white square was half-buried in the gravel and dirt. Stooping, she brushed the dirt away and picked it up and quickly examined it.

"It's just a piece of paper with rows and columns of numbers on it," Tony said impatiently, as he peered over her shoulder. "Forget about it, it's nothing."

"You're probably right." She stuffed it in her pocket. "Come on, let's go." Her thinking before had been to leave the past alone, not bothering to see any of her 1920s family and friends, and to get back to the present as soon as possible. Now she had changed her mind. It looked like Kami was in real danger and they needed adult help.

Moving quickly but quietly, Andrea led the way into the Forbidden tunnel. She was glad for the company this time, not feeling nearly as frightened as she had been before, although the walls still seemed to close in around her the further she walked.

The journey went much faster, and they soon found themselves walking out of the Forbidden tunnel into the larger tunnel that led to the train station. It seemed so wide and spacious after some of the other tunnels that it almost felt like walking above ground; almost, but not quite. This tunnel led to the train station, and it seemed much brighter than she remembered it.

Quickly scanning the walls, Andrea found the

source of the light – a huge lantern suspended from the dirt ceiling. What was that up there for? It appeared to have no real means of support and she couldn't figure out why it didn't just come crashing down on their heads. She was positive it hadn't been there before.

They stood for a moment looking south, trying to decide what to do next. "I was really hoping that Eddie would be hiding in the Forbidden tunnel," Andrea sighed, rubbing her forehead.

Suddenly the clumping sound of footsteps filled the tunnel. "Someone's coming from that way!" Tony pointed toward the train station.

"Hurry! Get into the Main Street Tunnel!" Andrea dashed into the tunnel, pulling Tony after her. They stood in the shadows, just out of sight as the noise got louder. Out of the gloom three figures took shape. One was a huge, beefy looking man with a mean glare. His left eye bulged out of its socket, causing his eyelid to be at half-mast across his eyeball. It was scary just looking at him. The second man was tall and skinny, and the third was a slight fellow, held captive between the other two.

The smaller figure struggled, trying to get free. "Let me go!"

"Is that Eddie?" Tony mouthed, his words barely audible.

Andrea studied the figure as the men passed by,

half pushing the smaller one along as they went. "I'm not sure, but it sounds like him." He was wearing the right clothes. The three men disappeared into the Forbidden tunnel in a flash, but not before the tall, skinny man turned and looked over his shoulder, his face toward Andrea.

Gasping, Andrea stepped back, quickly covering her mouth to block the sound. She was staring at Stilts, one of the men who had chased her through the tunnels during her first time travel adventure. She had run out on him and his rotund sidekick, Chubbs, after they had been trapped in a cave-in during her first visit to the tunnels two years before. She hoped that he couldn't see her.

"What are you kids doing in here?" a voice growled from behind.

Andrea whirled around and found herself staring at Chubbs. She ducked her head, hoping he wouldn't recognize her. "We-we-uhh –" she stuttered.

"We were just playing hide and seek," Tony said, thinking fast. "We – uh – we got lost."

Chubbs glared at them, raising his fist in their direction. "That'll teach ya for hanging around down here. I oughtta leave you here in the dark. Good thing Mean-Eyed Max didn't catch ya; you'd be in big trouble then." He laughed a cruel laugh that sent chills chasing down Andrea's spine, and she realized he was probably talking about the man with the scary-looking eye.

Chubbs's arms snaked out, grabbing Andrea and Tony roughly, forcing them to turn around and walk toward the Windy tunnel. This was taking them further and further from Eddie and Kami. Turning north at the intersection, they continued into the Windy tunnel, heading toward the Hazelton Hotel.

The tunnel was drafty, a faint wind blowing from the north. The lantern lights flickered, and Andrea almost hoped they would be extinguished. The surprise might give them a chance to get away from Chubbs and go back to looking for Eddie and Kami.

Just before the entrance to the Hazelton Hotel, Andrea spotted the belly tunnel she had once had to crawl through to warn Ol' Scarface of impending danger. It was bigger now, the earth hollowed out around it. Craning her neck, she peered at it, then poked Tony and gestured with her head, not wanting to attract the man's attention. He nodded as he stared at it too, then shrugged his shoulders. One belly tunnel was the same as all the rest, he thought.

"Quit yer wiggling, boy!" Chubbs commanded, squeezing Andrea's forearm until she cried out in pain. He jerked her forward. "I don't trust you," he whispered, thrusting her through the next tunnel entrance. "I was nice to you this time, but don't let me find you down here again, or else!"

Andrea wanted to scream and shout; kick him in the shins; but she knew that she would be overpowered within seconds. Her heart sinking lower and lower, she allowed herself to be pushed up a rickety spiral staircase to the surface. How could so many things have gone so badly so fast?

Oh no! Corrupt Cops?

Fresh air greeted them as Tony and Andrea were shoved out a small door in the side of the old Hazelton Hotel closest to Main Street. The wooden door was so well camouflaged against the brickwork of the building that it was almost lost from sight. "And don't come back!" Chubbs warned as the door clapped shut on his words.

Leaning against the side of the old brick building, legs shaking, Andrea took huge gulps of air and tried to think. What should they do now? Having just encountered those terrible men, she cringed at the idea of having to go back into the tunnels ever again. She didn't want to think about what would happen if they ran into Stilts, Chubbs, or Mean-Eyed Max again.

"Where are we?" Tony asked. He squinted down the street.

The sun had set and dusk was slowly enveloping the town. Looking around, Andrea saw the beginnings of Crescent Park just down the block. It looked very different from the modern-day park, with scraggly grass and a few bushes around the edges. Small trees had been planted here and there inside the park. She knew that these would flourish over the years, making a beautiful park in the heart of downtown Moose Jaw.

"We're at the Hazelton Hotel," she said, patting the warm bricks as she leaned against them. Their warmth helped calm her nerves. "See, there's the old warehouse where I was held captive last time," she said, pointing across Main to Ominica Street. Staring at the part of the building that fronted onto Main Street, Andrea squinted. "That's new," she commented quietly. "I don't remember a storefront in that warehouse building. 'Moose Jaw Laundry Service,'" she read slowly.

"That's where we lost Kami, right?" Tony asked.

"Yes," Andrea replied. "That underground storage area leads into the basement of the warehouse building. Rosie's house is just up the block from there. They must have taken us out another secret passage that leads directly up to the street. I didn't recognize it, though," she muttered, staring at the small wooden door set back from the street. It was almost lost in the dark shadows.

"I guess there are more tunnels around here than I realized. I especially don't remember using that creepy spiral stairway," she said, shuddering. "The steps were so worn, I thought I'd fall through!"

"We're in big trouble, Andrea," Tony whispered, tears beginning to well up in his eyes again. "What are we going to do? We lost both Kami and Eddie!"

Fighting back tears of her own, Andrea sighed, "I know. I hope they're okay."

"What do you think happened to them?" Tony asked, blinking rapidly to keep the tears back. "Do you think they really are slaves? How will they get free? I mean, did they make any money down there?"

"The indentured servants made a little bit. Most of those poor Chinese people had to scrimp and save for years to get enough money to pay the Head Tax. A lot of times they were only making twenty-five or thirty-five cents a day!"

"What?!" Tony blurted. "I get way more than that for allowance! They sure weren't treated fairly."

"You're right." Andrea's voice grew more passionate. "Even the government discriminated against the Chinese. It would only let the Chinese have certain jobs. They could run a restaurant or a tailor shop or a grocery store – that kind of thing. They couldn't be doctors or lawyers or teachers. They had to pay to bring their families to Canada! Sometimes the families were separated for years and years and kids grew up without seeing their fathers."

"That's really bad," Tony banged his fist into the palm of his hand, determination glinting in his blue eyes. "We have to get Kami and Eddie out of there!"

Andrea pushed away from the wall. "Let's go find Officer Paterson," she said. "He'll know what to do."

Movement caught her eye, drawing her gaze across the street to the old warehouse. Two men stood talking in the shadows. "Something's going on over there. That's the place they took Kami. Come on!" Under the cover of darkness they slipped quickly across Main Street and along Ominica behind a parked car, their eyes pinned on the men standing near the side door of the warehouse.

Curtained with the growing darkness of the night, the building looked as forbidding and scary as a haunted house. Andrea shivered. She remembered the terrible time she had spent in that warehouse last year. But surely the cops had cleaned it up, getting rid of all the bad guys and corruption that was going on there. Now it was just an old building, wasn't it?

They watched from behind the car as the two men headed toward Main Street, talking and laughing as they went. Tony jabbed Andrea in the stomach with his elbow. "Hey! They're cops!"

He was right, Andrea realized, keeping her eyes peeled on them. The men wore the dark uniforms of policemen, their heavy boots clunking on the ground as they walked. What had they been doing in the warehouse at this time of night?

Suddenly the side door sprang open. A tall, skinny man hurried through the door. "Hey!" He called after the policemen, waving something in the air. "You forgot this!"

Andrea pulled Tony back into the shadows. Not wanting to be seen, they crouched down again behind a parked car. "It looks like an envelope," Tony hissed in her ear.

Andrea was more concerned with the tall, skinny man. "There's Stilts again," she said, as she watched. "I wonder what he's up to. It's got to be no good, if he's involved." It looked as if the cops were working with the bad guys again.

"Thanks," the first policeman said, quickly taking the envelope from Stilts's hand and slipping it into the breast pocket in his uniform. "The other men would be angry if I didn't come back with this!" He tapped his pocket, making sure the envelope was secure.

"Sure, any time," Stilts said as he slipped back into the warehouse. "We always like doing business with you fellas. It helps our reputation."

The policeman laughed. "I want to get in on this deal," the second cop said.

"Any time," Stilts said leaning out the door. "We're always looking for happy clients." He shut the door as the cops strolled to Main Street, disappearing around the corner.

"What was that all about?" Tony wondered. "I can't figure it out."

"I can," Andrea breathed. Her worst fears were coming true. "The cops are doing corrupt things again. They're in business with the bad guys! I'm sure the envelope was full of money! Come on, let's follow them!" They raced to Main Street, carefully peering around the corner. "They're gone!" Andrea couldn't believe her eyes. "How could they have disappeared so quickly?"

"They must have another entrance to the tunnels, and they've gone back inside," Tony offered, feeling excitement rise in his body. He loved a mystery.

Andrea shivered, fear getting the best of her. "Let's go get Officer Paterson," she said, her mind replaying the scene with Stilts and the cops. It didn't make any sense.

She dragged Tony across Main street again, retracing their steps. "How could the cops have turned bad again?" Even the usually cheerful sight of the old post office clock shining forth in the twilight did nothing to lift her flagging spirits. They hurried down the side street toward the park. The fastest way was to go through the park, since the Talbot house stood across the street on the opposite side.

"Vance and Beanie will be home at this time of

night," Tony said, grinning in anticipation. "They'll sure be glad to see us!"

"And surprised," Andrea added. They crossed the dark grassland, being careful not to fall into any gopher holes. The last thing they needed was a twisted ankle, or worse.

"There's the house," Andrea pointed at the large structure, black against the night sky. No welcoming lights shone from inside the windows. "There's no one home." She sighed deeply as she stared at the house. Its gloomy appearance only added to her sad mood.

"Maybe they're all asleep," Tony tugged at her hand. "I'm getting really tired, Andrea."

"I know." She pulled him close to her side. "Me too."

"Let's just knock on the door and wake somebody up. They'll let us in. We're related, remember?"

Andrea agreed and stepped toward the edge of the park. Something moved in the shadows of the Talbot house. "Get down," she ordered, grabbing Tony by the hand and diving behind the bushes. "Someone's coming."

"You're getting paranoid," Tony groused, reluctantly allowing himself to be pulled behind the bushes. "It'll just be Vance or Officer Paterson."

It was the police, all right, but it wasn't Officer Paterson. The same two men they had seen at the warehouse just a few minutes earlier now skulked around Vance's house!

Tony stared at Andrea, his face lined with confusion and fear. "Do you think Constable Paterson is a bad guy now too?"

Andrea shrugged her shoulders. She was so confused she wasn't sure what to believe any more. "It's possible, I suppose," she said reluctantly, wondering if he could have turned to the dark side of the law. "It's not safe here. Let's go to Rosie's. She'll be able to help us. She'll know if Officer Paterson is still a good guy or not." Being as quiet as field mice, they crept away from the bushes. Their bodies blended into the shadows of the park as they moved silently over the prairie grass.

Lost in their own thoughts, feeling confused and betrayed, they trudged over to Ominica Street, toward Rosie's place. They were mute with worry, each afraid to voice the thoughts flitting around in their minds. What if Officer Paterson had been corrupted? Who could they depend on to help them?

"There's Grandpa Talbot's house," Tony pointed down the street. "I mean, Rosie's house," he amended. "Can you believe that we were just at a party here this afternoon and there were about a million people crammed inside? I wonder if the storm is over yet, back in our time?" Suddenly he wanted more than anything to be safely surrounded by his family, in the present.

They climbed the wide steps to the porch. "I hope

she's home," Andrea muttered, unable to ignore the feeling of apprehension still building inside her. Pushing open the wooden door, they stepped in, climbing the flights of stairs to Rosie's door. Andrea knocked softly.

They waited patiently on the steps, the only sound their breathing coming in excited puffs. "Try again," Tony suggested.

Andrea knocked once more, a little more firmly this time. After waiting a few seconds, she turned to face her brother, her eyebrows arched, her lips grim. "I don't think she's here right now."

"She has to be here." Tony reached around her and pounded on the door with his fist. "Open up, Rosie! It's me – Tony!"

"Sh-h-h," Andrea admonished, pushing his arm away from the door. "You don't want to disturb the neighbours."

Tony let his arm fall limply to his side. "I'm scared, Andrea," he admitted, moving down the stairs in front of her. "Nothing feels right this time. I think we're in big, big trouble here."

They reached the front porch. All of a sudden Andrea wanted nothing better than to sit down. Weary to the bone with exhaustion and worry, she slumped down onto the top step. "What if we just sit here for a while and wait? Maybe Rosie won't be that long; maybe she's working on a great story this late at night."

"But we don't even know if she still lives here," Tony said his voice weak.

Worried, Andrea studied his pale face. "When did you last eat?"

"I-I don't know –" he put a shaky hand to his forehead. "At the party sometime, I guess. I'm all confused, with the time-travel stuff and all."

"Well, eat something now," Andrea said, knowing that because of his diabetes he always carried food snacks in his backpack.

"Okay," Tony agreed, pulling his backpack off. Reaching into the sack, he found an almost endless supply of snacks. "Want something?"

Andrea shook her head. "No. I'm too upset to eat. I don't know what we're going to do. We don't have a clue what happened to Eddie or Kami and I'm really worried. This feels more dangerous than the last time we were here. I wish I knew what was going on. I wish I knew where everyone was. Rosie, Beanie, Vance, Officer Paterson, where are they?"

"What do we do now?' Tony asked, opening a package of granola and spilling some into his palm.

"I'm thinking..." A shiver of apprehension raced down Andrea's spine as she realized how very alone they were. Putting her head in her hands, she sighed, a long, heavy sound that filled the night air with all of their unvoiced worries. What if there was no one to help them? It looked as if she and Tony would have to figure out how to rescue the Mark twins all on their own.

LIFE IN THE LAUNDRY

Kami screamed at the top of her lungs, kicking ineffectually at the men who held her captive. She was so light, they easily pulled her through a heavy wooden door, her toes barely touching the ground. The door slammed shut behind them and she found herself being dragged through a large warehouse.

"Shut up, coolie!" an angry voice thundered near her ear as rough hands shook her. Terrified, her vocal cords froze as fear squeezed her throat closed. The only sound was her breath, panting out in sharp gasps as her heart thundered in her ears.

Questions and terrifying thoughts bombarded her brain as the men pulled her across the large open area. Where was she? What did these men want? And why had one of them called her coolie? She remembered hearing that term somewhere before, but where? It wasn't a nice thing to say, she could tell by the sneering tone of his voice.

Kicking was futile and only made the men treat her more roughly. "Settle down, coolie," the same mean voice advised. "If you know what's good for you."

They've kidnapped me. The thought reverberated around her panic-stricken brain and she began to shake. Overpowered by the men, Kami quit thrashing about, going limp in their grasp. She tried to think of a way to escape, but her brain was a petrified mass of fear.

Two of the men still held her, hurrying her across the floor. Another raced ahead to a door half hidden in the wall. He pulled it open and disappeared inside. Kami suddenly became aware of a strong odour hanging in the air. It smelled of bleach and soap and fried vegetables. As she neared the door, it grew stronger, filling her lungs. What was that stench?

With two men pushing her from above, and one reaching for her from below, Kami had no choice but to obey. The smell was overpowering, causing tears to form in her eyes. She could barely see where she was going. Loud thumping noises and piercing hisses registered in her brain as the men escorted her a short distance across the basement floor to another door. Pushing it open, they dragged her inside, pushing her to her knees. The noise was almost deafening and the odour made her cough. Wiping the tears away with her sleeve, she stared, her eyes huge.

Coughing and choking, she stared out at the sights around her, trying to take everything in at once. People dressed much as she was ran about the area, totally ignoring her and the three dangerous-looking men who had brought her here. It was as if this was an everyday occurrence!

Several large vats of steaming water stood in a row, workers bending over them. Ancient looking ironing boards stood near large furnaces. Long cords of rope were strung across the low ceilings with clothes draped over them. Some of the people were ironing things; some were hanging clothes, others lifted steaming bunches of material out of the large vats, using long sticks. It looked like an old fashioned laundry! Who were all these people?

Oppressive heat wrapped itself, moist and sticky, around Kami's body. Between the heat and the smell, she began to feel light-headed. She put her hand over her nose and mouth, trying to filter out the terrible smell. It should have been poisonous, and yet the other people didn't even seem to notice it.

Where am I? her brain kept asking. She had heard of something like this, she realized, but her scared brain wouldn't cooperate and she couldn't remember where or when. She felt like Alice in Wonderland, suddenly caught in another world. Nothing was making sense down here.

At the back of the laundry area, almost hidden from view, was a kitchen. Several crude wooden tables stood in a row, long benches stretching along either side of them. Two large, old-fashioned stoves had been placed against the far wall. Huge steaming pots were on the stoves, an older man busily stirring them, his back to the commotion going on around him.

To Kami's left was a raised platform. A small office had been built on it, its large windows overseeing the work area. Two of the men stood on the platform talking to another man who seemed to be in charge of this underground nightmare. The third man had been left to stand guard over her. She could feel the toe of his left boot digging into her thigh.

The boss studied Kami from a distance, then nodded, handing money to the shorter man. "We got our due," the short man called loudly over the din of machines, pocketing the money as he made his way back toward her. "Here's the safe delivery of another worker. She must have got away from the last bunch. Now let's get out of here; we have another shipment to take to a grocery store in town." They disappeared through the door they had come in, without a backward glance, slamming it shut behind them.

"You, over there!" A loud voice roared and Kami jumped. "Come over here." He beckoned with his hand and she knew he was talking to her. Reluctantly she got to her feet and moved unsteadily across the floor. She really had no choice but to follow orders until she figured out where she was and what was going on. The cap jiggled precariously on her head, and she pushed it firmly back in place, surprised that she still had it after all she'd been through.

"You're new," the man said, waving at one of the workers. A tall boy not much older than Kami came over. He looked like a taller, skinnier version of Eddie. "You teach the new person the ropes, Jimmy." Nodding, Jimmy bowed slightly as the man continued.

"Stanford's my name," the man told Kami. Pointing to his chest he repeated, "Stanford. And don't get any idea about escaping. The doors are blocked, guarded." He was speaking slowly, his hands gesturing toward the doors, his fingers entwining to imitate a lock. It's like he thinks I don't understand English, she thought.

"You stick with Jimmy," he added, pointing to the boy. "You'll do okay. No trouble, mind." He jabbed a long finger under Kami's chin. "I don't want trouble here. We don't take kindly to coolies causing problems; mysterious things have happened to troublemakers." He grinned menacingly at her. "Got a name?"

Kami's tongue was frozen to the roof of her mouth, her throat dry and scratchy. She opened her mouth, but no sound came out. He was threatening her!

"Name," Stanford repeated. He jabbed his finger into his chest. "Stanford," he said, slowly pronouncing the word. Pointing at Jimmy he said, "Jimmy." He pointed expectantly at Kami.

"K-K-Kami," she finally managed to stutter between stiff lips.

"Show Kami the ropes," he ordered, and Jimmy bowed again as Stanford turned on his heel and walked away.

Jimmy smiled, escorting her past the machines and into the kitchen area. He said a few words but Kami didn't catch any of it. "Pardon," she said, leaning closer to hear him. When he spoke again, Kami watched his mouth move, his lips twisting out the foreign words, his voice rising and falling lyrically. He had obviously done this many times before and Kami wondered how many other people he had 'shown the ropes' and why? What was this place? What was she doing here?

Panic gripped Kami's stomach. Where was she? It must be a hoax. She had been expecting to hear English words. It took her a moment to realize the boy who was smiling kindly at her was speaking Chinese!

EDDIE'S ESCAPE

Eddie was being pushed along by Mean-Eyed Max, his arms twisted painfully behind his back. He was being kidnapped! But why?! They were walking through tunnels, just like the ones Andrea and Tony were so sure were underground in Moose Jaw. Could this be real? He must be having a nightmare!

"Get moving, coolie!" Mean-Eyed Max snarled, his breath fanning across the back of Eddie's neck. "I ain't got all day to take you back where you belong." He twisted Eddie's arm even tighter. He walked with a funny gait, his huge size making it awkward for him to move in the low tunnel. Even though he was hunched over, his head almost brushed the roof, while his knees bent at what looked to be a painful angle.

Eddie opened his mouth to speak, but shock and

terror froze his vocal cords. His tongue wagged but no sound was emitted. "You coolies are all alike, coming to our country, taking our money for your own gain."

Totally confused, Eddie wondered what was he talking about. He had only heard the word coolie once before and it was during the tour of the tunnels his class had taken last year. It was a racist term that had been used in the 1900s to describe Chinese people. Where was he? What was going on?

Mean-Eyed Max stumbled as they neared the intersection of tunnels. Before he even thought about it, Eddie had taken action. Catching the bad guy off balance, he shoved him as hard as he could, throwing him against the tunnel wall.

Already at an awkward angle, Mean-Eyed Max fell like a ton of bricks, the weight of his body causing an avalanche of dirt and pebbles to fall from the roof. He was quick, though; his arm snaked out, grabbing Eddie's ankle, his fingers wrapping around it in a vise grip of anger. "You're in trouble now, coolie!" Spit spewed in the air around him as Mean-Eyed Max raged.

Truly terrified for his life, Eddie tried to leap backward. His right ankle was still trapped in Mean-Eyed Max's strong hand and Eddie was thrown off balance. His left leg flew up and the toe of his shoe caught Mean-Eyed Max right on the knee. A loud howl of pain echoed around him as Mean-Eyed Max grabbed his leg in pain, and Eddie knew he was in big trouble. Wrenching himself free, he raced away, leaving Mean-Eyed Max clutching his knee in pain.

Eddie knew he had to hide, but where? He was totally lost and confused. Where was he? Now was no time to worry about that, though. His first concern was trying to get out of this mess. There didn't seem to be any place to hide. Up ahead he saw a smaller tunnel, the darkness reaching out toward him. He headed into the smaller tunnel, engulfed in the void within seconds.

Eddie could feel the top of his head brush against the tunnel ceiling. The darkness was complete. He couldn't even see his feet as they raced over the uneven earth. He came upon a sputtering lantern, weak rings of light pooling on the ground. Pausing, he leaned against the dirt wall, his heart hammering in his chest. Was he being followed? Silence drummed in his ears and he realized he was alone. Where am I? he asked over and over in his agitated mind. Oh, what was going on?

The need to know something about his situation drove him back the way he had come. Cautiously Eddie crept back through the small tunnel. Sounds of someone grunting in pain reached his ears. Mean-Eyed Max obviously wasn't moving too fast right now. Eddie's confidence nudged up a notch, and he peered out of the blackness and into the tunnel intersection.

Limping badly, Mean-Eyed Max swore a string of words that would have made Eddie's grandmother cringe in horror. "Where'd that coolie go?" he muttered to himself. He stared into the inky blackness of the Forbidden tunnel where Eddie stood just out of sight. "I haven't got time to chase after you now! You'd think a guy would want to work for a while, make some money. You sure can't do any favours for these coolies; they're never satisfied!"

Eddie's heart jumped in his throat as he listened, but he remained as still as a deer trapped in headlights. He could see every detail of Mean-Eyed Max's pained face, but he was sure Mean-Eyed Max couldn't see him.

Mean-Eyed Max hobbled toward the Forbidden tunnel, then clutched his knee. He cursed loudly, kicking the ground with his good leg. "I'm not done with you yet, coolie!" He waved his powerful fist toward the Forbidden tunnel and shook it, his eyes wild. Eddie felt the threat in the pit of his stomach and prayed that he would never run into this man again.

A low-hanging lantern swung from the tunnel ceiling. Eddie watched as Mean-Eyed Max reached up and pulled on the lantern. As it moved toward the ground, a section of the tunnel began to lift away from the wall. It was a secret entrance!

The bad guy lifted the door just enough to allow

his hulking body to squeeze inside. Casting one more glare toward the Forbidden tunnel, Mean-Eyed Max disappeared, the lantern moving back into place as the door settled against the tunnel wall. Who would have guessed that there was an entrance there?

Cautiously Eddie moved out into the area, coming to stand beneath the low hanging lantern. His first impulse was to follow Mean-Eyed Max, to find out where he was going. This might give him a clue as to where he was and what was going on. Standing underground in what was obviously a tunnel system, he was pretty sure he already knew. Maybe there really were tunnels in Moose Jaw. Even though Eddie didn't want to believe it, it sure seemed real. But who were these bad guys? Why were they so mean and why was he called a coolie?

Nearby a piece of paper lay against the tunnel wall. Eddie picked it up, smoothing it out to study it. He held it up to the lantern, angling it to catch the light. The old-fashioned print jumped out at him as he stared at the words. It was a flyer advertising a sale at The Moose Jaw Hardware Store. The headline read: "Keep the Lawn Green." He read aloud, not quite believing the words, "Lawn mowers: nine dollars, twelve dollars, fourteen dollars. Fifty-foot hose: eight dollars; sprinkling cans: one dollar and fifty cents!" The address was given, along with the strangest phone number Eddie had ever seen. It was only four digits long!

Slumping against the wall, Eddie clumsily folded the paper with numb fingers, slipping it into his pocket. Once he had heard Tony say something stupid about time travel. Was it possible? Had he and Kami been dragged back in time? No, it wasn't possible! It must be some kind of joke, and he was going to find out what it was all about!

Eddie grabbed the lantern and pulled. The secret door opened just enough for him to slide underneath. It settled back behind him and he found himself once again in suffocating blackness. Feeling as if he was suspended in space, Eddie inched his way forward, his hands reaching out to guide him along. His fingers knocked tiny pebbles off the walls of the tunnel. They fell to the floor, the sounds flowing around him as he moved. Every nerve in his body was on high alert. His scalp tingled in fear as his eyes bored into the void. He wasn't sure how much longer he could stomach being totally alone in this nothingness.

Eddie was almost at the point of turning back when he became aware of sounds filtering through the tunnel. He moved on slowly, the noises growing more distinct. Footsteps, he decided. He could hear the steady sound of footsteps as they marched across a floor. Where was it coming from?

The sounds of steady walking reached out to him, drawing him closer. He could just see the faint outline of a door, light tracing its dimensions in the darkness.

Putting his hand on the knob, he waited a moment. Should he open it? Fear almost swallowing him whole, he did the only thing he could. Carefully turning the knob, he gently pulled on the door and peeked inside.

A large room with a low ceiling was full of tables. About a dozen men marched up and down a crudely built set of stairs. They would climb the stairs empty-handed and return with heavy wooden boxes balanced on their shoulders. They looked like the kind of boxes fruit and vegetables used to come in.

Mean-Eyed Max stood in a corner of the room talking and gesturing to a man in a suit. The men carrying the boxes ignored him, but Eddie studied them closely. They were all Chinese, their faces grim, eyes downcast, as they carried the heavy wooden crates down the stairs.

One man tripped, the box crashing to the steps. Apples erupted from the box, bouncing down the stairs. The worker scrambled to his feet. Picking up the crate, he hurried to gather the fruit. "Be careful, coolie!" the man in the suit yelled, as he poked the worker with a long stick and then brought it down hard on a nearby table. A loud crack thundered through the air as the workers cringed. "Don't bruise the fruit! I can sell it for five cents a pound right now! It's worth more than you are!"

Five cents a pound? Apples for five cents a pound?! A cold finger of realization ran down his back. He must have gone back in time! Dread and disbelief filled his paralyzed body. Could it be true? It must be, he decided. Why else would people be treated so badly? He watched as the man in the suit walked between the Chinese people, threatening them with the stick if he thought they weren't working hard or fast enough.

Upset at what he saw, Eddie's first impulse was to rush in and rescue the poor worker. Disgust and indignation made him forget to be quiet. He yanked the door so hard it nearly fell off its hinges and was halfway across the room before he thought about Mean-Eyed Max. What had happened to him?

A red-hot hand clamped itself around his neck and squeezed. Turning around, Eddie met the angry glare of Mean-Eyed Max. "I knew you'd follow me," he breathed, his eyes piercing Eddie's soul. "Stupid coolies, you think you're so smart. I'm going to teach you a lesson you'll never forget."

Dangling from the man's hard grasp, his toes barely reaching the ground, realization flooded into Eddie's brain. He now knew for certain he was back in time in the tunnels in Moose Jaw! Warm, putrid breath fanned his frozen features as the hand on his neck began to tighten. The man with the rod was coming across the room and Eddie had no chance to escape. He was caught like a rabbit in a trap and just as petrified.

TROUBLE ON MAIN STREET

"Let's go find somewhere to sleep," Andrea finally said, nudging Tony off the step. "I wonder if they close the train station for the night?" She had been wracking her brain, trying to figure out where they could spend the night. "At least we'd be warm on those long wooden benches." It was a good idea, and they walked quickly to Main Street and turned south toward the station. Its bright light drew them like moths to a candle; the only welcoming they had felt since arriving back in time.

"Think it'll be open?" Tony asked, shuffling along beside her, his backpack safely on his back.

"I hope so," Andrea said, hurrying ahead.

All she could think about was finding Kami and Eddie fast and trying to get back to the present. They didn't belong to the past, and her biggest fear was that they would somehow get stuck back in time forever. What would it be like to become a woman of the 1920s? Inconvenient, she decided. She'd been looking forward to owning her own cell phone and driving the family car with air conditioning and a CD player. Somehow, driving those Model T-type cars of the 1920s wouldn't be the same at all. And anyway, did they even let women drive?!

The huge and reassuring sight of the train station, at the very end of Main Street, lifted her spirits. Even at this distance, it looked impressive as it stood overlooking the town, the luminous clock face shining brightly. Andrea could understand why this was her father's favourite building in all of Moose Jaw.

"Where do you think everyone is?" Tony asked again for what seemed the hundredth time. "I miss them." He put his hand into Andrea's, drawing comfort.

"I don't know," Andrea sighed. "I wish I did."

They came to River Street and a flurry of quiet activity halfway down the block caught their attention. "What's going on?" Tony asked.

They turned the corner, drawn by the strange sight of so many people working so late at night. An antique truck with spoke wheels and wooden frames for sides was backed up to a business. Men scurried back and forth like ants, unloading boxes from the truck.

Andrea grabbed Tony, pulling him back into the shadow of the building near the corner. "We don't want to be seen," she warned quietly. "If they're doing this at night, it's probably illegal."

They watched for a few minutes, their backs pressed against the stone building. The bricks were still warm from the hot afternoon and felt cozy on their tired bodies.

"Those people are all Chinese," Tony pointed out, staring along the street. They could hear a foreman yelling orders as the workers carried the heavy boxes into the building. One of the workers was escorted out of the building by Stilts and Chubbs. "Hey! That looks like Eddie!"

It was Eddie! Andrea was sure of it! Excited to finally find someone they knew, Andrea didn't stop to think. Cupping her hands to her mouth she yelled as loudly as she could, "Eddie!" The sound echoed up and down the street as the workers froze. Stilts and Chubbs whipped their heads around following the sound.

"Oh no," Andrea breathed, covering her trembling lips with ice-cold fingers. "What have I done?" Not bothering to find out, she grabbed Tony's hand. "Run!"

Andrea and Tony raced back to Main Street, the sound of shouts and pounding feet racing toward them. Careening around the corner, they collided with two solid bodies and were sent sprawling to the ground. Arms and legs hopelessly tangled, they lay in a heap on the sidewalk as the footsteps moved closer and closer.

Grunting and groaning, Andrea tried to sort out which arms and legs were hers. "Watch where you're going next time," a deep voice growled. It sounded vaguely familiar, but Andrea was too scared to try to figure out whose voice it was.

"Sorry," she sputtered, her mind on the sound of running feet behind her.

"Come on," the same person said, quickly getting up and pulling her along with him. "Get up, kiddo! Let's get out of here! If you want to stay out of trouble, follow us!"

Not bothering to question where they were going, Andrea and Tony hurried after them. Andrea was sure the men would come surging around the corner and be upon them within seconds. Wherever they were going, it had to be safer than standing on Main Street!

Partway up the next block, the pair in front suddenly veered into the shadows of a building and promptly disappeared. "Hey! Where'd they go?" Tony demanded, peering down the sidewalk.

"I don't know," Andrea replied, hope fading within her. They'd be caught for sure now, stuck in the middle of the block like misplaced wildlife.

"Psst, down here." To her right, against the building, was a narrow circular staircase. It led down to the basement level of the building, which had an outside entrance. At night, deep in the shadows of the building, it wasn't visible. Andrea and Tony leapt down the stairs, diving into the furthest corner, under the winding stairs, just as the men flew past.

"Keep back and out of sight," a voice whispered into the darkness, and four bodies pressed as far under the circular staircase as they could go. Had Andrea been paying attention, she might have recognized the voice, but all of her senses were pinned on the men on the sidewalk.

"We lost 'em," Stilts panted as his footsteps slowed to a walk.

"They're around here somewhere," Chubbs growled. "They couldn't have run that fast. Find 'em!" The men fanned out, some crossing to the other side of the street, their footsteps echoing eerily in the deserted roadway.

"I'll take a closer look here." Stilts sounded to be directly above Andrea's head. She listened, her scalp tingling in fear, as the sound of a footstep clunked on the first step. He was coming down the stairs! Holding her breath, her heart jumping into her throat, she pushed her body as far back into the corner as possible. She felt the pressure of the others packed tightly against her. Her nose was pressed against a soft-brimmed cap much like her own. Its dusty smell filled her nostrils and her nose began to twitch. She hoped she wouldn't sneeze. She could feel someone's pulse beating wildly under her sweaty palms; was it hers?

Stilts was halfway down the staircase, his shoes clearly visible between the steps. Andrea could have reached through the open steps to touch his pant legs. Her nose burned with the need to sneeze and she wiggled it, willing the feeling away. If only she could free her hands to rub it. The man turned, as if to go and she sighed with relief.

The sneeze came so suddenly, Andrea wasn't even sure it came from her. The sound seemed to explode into the darkness like the crisp sound of a gunshot. She watched in horror as the man jumped swiftly down two more steps, his liquid movements melting into the shadows around him. They were caught!

Just as his foot hit the last step, a siren wailed nearby. "Police!" someone yelled. "Let's get out of here." The man hesitated for a moment, standing stock-still on the last step. Then his foot pivoted on the cement stair and he swiftly mounted the steps and was gone.

"That was close," Andrea said, air rushing out of her lungs. She extricated herself from the pressing bodies and shook her arms to get the blood moving again.

"Who sneezed?" the same deep voice asked, anger just below the surface.

"I-I did," Andrea stuttered. "I couldn't help it."

"We're just lucky the police siren got his attention, or we'd all have been done for."

The voice sounded very familiar and Andrea peered into the darkness, but the figure was still back in the shadows and unrecognizable. "Thank you for rescuing us," she said. Maybe these people could help them, if she played her cards right. Mounting the stairs, she moved toward the light.

"Andrea?" a soft voice questioned, the smaller person peering at her to get a better look. "Tony?"

WHO ARE YOU?

"Beanie! Vance! It's you!" Andrea felt tears of relief fill her eyes as she flew back down the stairs. She threw herself at Beanie, wrapping her arms around her. "I thought we wouldn't find you. I was so worried."

"I knew I recognized that sneeze," Vance grumbled good-naturedly. He grabbed Tony, pounding him on the back so hard that he almost knocked him off his feet.

Tony reciprocated, grabbing Vance around the chest in a gigantic bear hug. "Hiya, Grandpa," he teased, a huge grin on his face.

Vance pretended to box him on the ears. "I told you not to call me that," he smiled back. They traded partners and the hugging continued with Vance awkwardly patting Andrea on the back as they stood in the shadow of the stairs.

"I'm so glad to see you!" Stretching up, Andrea found she had to stand on tiptoes to reach her arms around Vance's neck. He had grown so tall. And Beanie too, had grown. She was much taller, her legs gangly and thin.

The sound of the siren grew louder as it wailed down Main Street. "We'd better get out of here," Vance said, climbing the steps to the street and peering this way and that. "The coast is clear," he said. "Let's hightail it over to the park." Four young bodies sprinted across Main Street and onto the side street, deserted at this time of night.

They came to a stop under a small tree and fell to their knees, breathing in large gulps of cool night air. "I'm so glad to see you," Beanie smiled, leaning against Andrea's arm.

"Me too," Andrea replied, hugging her close. "We were beginning to think you'd left town or something. We went to your house and no one was there."

"But we saw cops snooping around! What's going on?" Tony asked.

"Our parents have gone on a honeymoon of sorts," Vance explained. "Ma wanted Beanie to stay with Rosie, but since she's out of town right now, I get to babysit." He grimaced. "It's not a job I'm fond of, especially when I keep having to track her down at night!" He wagged his finger under her nose. "You're supposed to stay home, not go gallivanting all over Moose Jaw! It's dangerous out here at night!"

Beanie grinned innocently. "I was just out taking a walk."

"A likely story," Vance muttered. "Stay home next time!"

"But what about the cops at your place?" Tony insisted.

"Oh, they were just checking up on us and the house, making sure there were no problems. They probably thought Beanie and I were in bed asleep, like most people are at this time of night!" Vance glared at her.

"Vance isn't home very much," Beanie quickly threw in, cleverly turning the attention away from herself. "He's working a lot, aren't you, Vance?"

He nodded happily. "I'm really busy selling newspapers. I've worked my way up in the business too," Vance said proudly, sitting up taller and puffing out his chest.

How self-assured Vance sounded, Andrea reflected, gazing at him thoughtfully. He certainly had changed since the first time she had met him two summers ago.

"What are you doing now?" Tony asked.

"I run errands for the boss and they let me set the type. I'm not fast yet, but I soon will be. Mr. Smith says I have a way with words, just like Rosie. He wants me to do some writing on my own and show it to him, and maybe he'll put an article of mine in the paper someday."

"Wow," Andrea said softly. She wasn't convinced about the reason Vance gave for the cops being at his house so late at night, but she didn't voice her doubts. "So, are you writing at home?" Suddenly he seemed like a stranger, this tall, mature boy with a strong male voice. She didn't know how to act around him. "Are you any good at it?"

Vance shrugged modestly. "I don't know yet. Anyway, that's Rosie's department, but she's away just now." He brushed her question aside, looking as if he regretted saying so much. It was strange hearing him talk about writing. She didn't remember her grandpa ever talking about that.

"So that explains it," Tony said, interrupting her thoughts. "Where did Rosie go? We were really beginning to get worried. We thought we were back in time without our friends."

Vance beamed, a huge smile lighting his face. "Never fear, we're here!" He chuckled and continued. "Rosie was invited to work for the Regina *Morning Leader* for a month. It's a great opportunity for her, and she's teaching other women how to be good newspaperwomen while she's there. She writes home often, telling us all about her adventures —"

"And we write back, telling her all about how boring things are in Moose Jaw," Beanie broke in. "But now all that's about to change!" She grabbed Tony's arm, pulling him to his feet, and spun him around in a circle, laughing merrily. "I'm so glad you're here!"

"Why are you here?" Vance questioned, ignoring the younger two. His eyes bored into Andrea's.

In all the excitement and danger, Andrea had momentarily forgotten about Eddie and Kami. "We got sent back in time to help two of our friends. They got sent here too, but we can't find them. I think they're in real danger."

"Danger! Excitement!" Beanie beamed, rubbing her hands together. "I can't wait to hear all about it! What's going on?"

As briefly as possible, Andrea filled them in on Kami and Eddie. She described how Kami had been grabbed by some men and forced into the old warehouse and how they had gone to look for Eddie and thought they'd recognized him being dragged away by the bad guys.

"We don't know where either of them are," Andrea finished, looking worried. "We saw a great big ugly man called Mean-Eyed Max with Stilts and Eddie. Tony and I didn't have a chance to follow him. Chubbs came up behind us and escorted us out of the tunnels, through the Windy tunnel and out a rickety old staircase at the Hazelton Hotel. Eddie could be anywhere in Moose Jaw by now, and so could Kami."

"You met Mean-Eyed Max?" Beanie's eyes grew huge with fear. "He's the scariest man in all of Moose Jaw, and not just because of his glass eye, either. Some people say he killed a man with his bare hands just because he disagreed with him. They say he lost his real eye in a fight and that his false eye bulges out like that because his real eye just got pushed back inside his head." She shuddered. "I hate looking at him."

"This is serious," Vance interrupted, absently rubbing his chin while he sat deep in thought. "I wonder what Mean-Eyed Max is up to? Wherever he is, trouble isn't too far behind."

"Do you know him?" Andrea asked, shivering in spite of herself.

"Yeah, I know him," Vance said curtly. "He seems to have taken over where Ol' Scarface left off. He's big and mean and dangerous. Stay out of his way," he warned, his voice gruff with concern.

"But he took Eddie," Tony cried. "We have to rescue him!"

"What are their names again?" Vance asked.

"Kami and Eddie Mark," Andrea replied. "They're twins and they're fourteen years old."

"Mark?" Vance questioned. "Isn't that a Chinese name?"

"Yes," Andrea confirmed.

"Chinese!" Beanie exclaimed. "Oh no!" she moaned, her voice full of worry. "Chinese people aren't treated very well in Moose Jaw sometimes. They probably won't find too many friendly faces around. They could be in danger. I heard Sylvia's Pa say that some Chinese people live and work in the tunnels, hiding from the police. They get treated really badly down there because they can't tell on the bad guys for doing mean things to them."

"I don't believe it's as bad as all that." Vance stood up, dusting off the seat of his trousers. "And anyway, I thought the tunnels had been boarded up."

"If it's not all that bad, then why are we here?" Tony demanded, firing questions at Vance. "Why did they kidnap Kami? And where's Eddie?"

"There is something going on in the tunnels," Andrea insisted. "Those men were frightening, and they were definitely up to no good."

"Andrea says that Kami and Eddie are going to become indentured servants, living and working in the tunnels," Tony blurted. "I think they're going to be slaves!"

"Servants? Slaves?" Vance shook his head. "You're letting your imagination get away with you, Tony. I've never seen any evidence of Chinese people as...as slaves or servants. And I'd know it too. After all, I used to be a tunnel runner!" His blue eyes flashed with indignation as he looked around the group. "I'd know if something fishy was going on. What you're saying is all hogwash."

"Hogwash?" Tony questioned, a frown knitting his eyebrows. "What does that mean?"

"It means it's garbage, lies, falsehoods. It's just a myth." Vance folded his arms indignantly across his chest. "I don't believe a word of it."

"Well," Andrea sighed, nonplussed by Vance's attitude, "whether you believe it or not, something has happened to Kami and Eddie and we need to find them. You will help us, won't you, Vance?"

The night was silent. Everyone sat as frozen as ice sculptures on a frigid prairie morning, wondering what Vance would say. Andrea didn't know what she would do if he didn't agree to help them.

"If Officer Paterson were here, he'd help us," Tony said confidently, forgetting the scene he and Andrea had just witnessed at the darkened house.

The stillness of the night seemed to stretch into eternity until Vance finally spoke. "All right," he sighed, shaking his head. "Looks like I'm the only one around here who can help you. After all, I'm the oldest, and someone's got to be in charge."

Andrea got to her feet and reached out to squeeze his hand. "Thank you, Vance. I don't think Tony and I could do it on our own. We need your help." He smiled at her as he patted her shoulder. When he smiled like that, he looked just like Grandpa Talbot, and that made her heart glad.

Tony yawned widely, rubbing tired eyes. "I've had enough excitement for one night," he told them. "I'm ready for bed. Where are we going to sleep?"

Kami Gets a Job

Kami lay on a makeshift bed staring up at the ceiling beams directly above. They were a mere twenty centimetres from her nose. She'd have to be careful when she sat up; it would be easy to hit her head. All around her people slept, their snores and sighs mingling in the dank air. She lay there on the top bunk because she didn't know what else to do.

The last few hours had been a blur of confusion and bewilderment, not to mention terror. She'd finally figured out that if she did what they wanted her to do, they left her alone. The Chinese people had been very nice, especially Jimmy, who had taken her under his wing, showing her around. He had chattered on in his language, pointing to this and that, leading her around the cluttered area. "Don't you speak English?"

Kami had finally asked in desperation.

He had stared at her blankly at first and she had repeated. "English. Do you speak English?"

Surprise and alarm had dashed across Jimmy's face and he had quickly placed a finger over her lips to silence her. He had shaken his head solemnly and pointed to Stanford, and Kami had gotten the message. She would be very careful not to let Stanford know she spoke English.

Jimmy had led her around the laundry area, showing her the large vats of steaming water, the washboards that looked like corrugated cardboard, the heavy old-fashioned irons kept on a special metal shelf on nearby furnaces, and the endless lines of rope strung overhead. He was showing her the jobs, she realized, when he mimicked ironing on a rickety wooden ironing board that stood near the blazing furnace.

No wonder it was so deadly hot and humid in here, she thought. Between the heat blasting from the squat furnaces and the boiling water in the vats, it was a virtual sauna. Everyone's forehead glistened with perspiration. Kami could feel it beading on her upper lip and she wiped it away with her sleeve. She was glad to see that there were women as well as men working here. Although there were more men, having the women smile at her helped. She didn't feel quite so alone.

After that, Jimmy turned into a narrow hallway beside the large stoves, gesturing as he went. He wanted her to follow him. The hallway led to the living area, which held a sea of bunk beds standing in rows the length and width of the room. They were stacked three beds high. Pieces of rough wood had been nailed on the end, the only ladder for climbing up and getting into bed. It was downright scary, having to climb two beds high before bending over the top bar and falling into bed. Kami wondered how she would ever get down again. She hadn't gotten brave enough to try it yet.

Dinner had been gross, almost inedible to her modern palate. It was a thin, grey soup and bowls of rice. A huge soup bowl had been put in the middle of the table, smaller bowls of rice placed around it. Thrusting chopsticks into her numb fingers, Jimmy had directed her to help set the table for the workers. He hurriedly placed two sizes of small bowls in each spot. She realized later that the smallest bowl was for tea.

Kami watched, fascinated, as the workers came quickly to the tables, filled their bowls with rice or soup and began to eat. Those eating rice first used the chopsticks, holding the bowls up to their mouths. The ones eating soup drank it from the bowls.

Washing a ton of dishes was her second job. She had plunged her hands repeatedly into the hot water, her skin puckering and turning red. The others had rushed back to their work even though it was evening.

It was as if they worked eighteen hours a day down here. After what seemed like an eternity, they had quit working, the noises growing softer as the workers tripped off to bed. Exhausted, they fell asleep within moments, their bodies still.

Now was the perfect chance to escape! Feeling sure everyone was asleep, Kami scooted to the end of the bed and looked down. Three beds high was a long way down, and she suddenly felt dizzy. Getting into the bed had been relatively easy; getting out would be more difficult.

On a wing and a prayer, desperation making her leave the bed, she lay on her back and swung her legs up and over the top piece of wood. Gripping it with both hands, she scooted along until her buttocks rested on the bar. This wouldn't work at all, she realized, her whole body perched on one small board. She was stuck, paralyzed by the fear of heights.

Prying tense fingers from the board, she drew her right arm across her body, grabbing the board on her left. Hanging on for dear life, she twisted, her legs flailing out in panic as she caught the top board with her left hand and turned her body around, her stomach heaving against the bar.

Frantically, Kami searched for the foothold. Her toe brushed something solid and she tested it before putting her full weight on it. That was it. Breathing a sigh of relief, she continued her climb down, realizing that every time she got out of that bed she'd have to repeat the same process. She hurried through the narrow hallway and out the darkened entrance, stopping beside the huge stoves.

Standing alone in the laundry area, the murmurs and snorts of the other workers barely reaching her ears, she realized how old-fashioned and authentic everything looked. An awful thought popped into her mind. Had they really gone back in time? People didn't time travel; they couldn't. It was only possible in the movies, right? She had finally let that terrorizing thought come into her brain. Everything seemed real, including Jimmy and the other workers. And Stanford, with his harsh words and mean ways, was real too.

Her first thought was to escape the way she had come. The door stood several metres away, at the end of the laundry area. What would she find outside the door? Was it safe for her to travel back through the warehouse? What kinds of horrors might she encounter?

Gathering all her courage, Kami drew herself upright and bolted for the door. She didn't care what was on the other side, she only wanted out of this living nightmare. She reached the door and turned the knob, pulling on it. Nothing happened. She pulled again, this time with all her strength. The door remained closed. It was locked and she didn't have a key. Now what?

Turning around, Kami studied Stanford's office. It looked deserted. That was where she might discover something that would either alleviate or confirm her worst fears.

Quickly scanning the area, she stole forward. On feet feather-soft, she tiptoed toward the office, her eyes straining to watch for any movement, her ears listening for any different sound. Fear gripped her stomach, for she didn't know where Stanford was.

The need to know pushed her forward and she mounted the three wooden stairs, her hand clutching the rail to take some of her weight. She didn't want any sudden creaks to alert anyone to her presence in forbidden places. Gliding across the platform, a small apparition in white, she stared in through the window. The glow from the laundry area produced enough light for her to see inside, and she pressed her nose against the glass to get a better look.

A huge desk was pushed up against the window, its top littered with papers. Behind it stood a big wooden desk chair. Across the small room, deep in the shadows, was a cot, but Kami couldn't tell if it was occupied or not. A small braided rug lay on the floor beside it, giving the room an almost cozy appeal, and she wondered if this was Stanford's only home.

With a heavy sigh, Kami began to turn away from the window. She didn't know what she'd expected, but she had hoped for a sign or a clue to tell her what was going on. A newspaper lay folded up on the edge of the desk. Something about it caught Kami's attention and she turned again, her nose pressed against the glass, warm breath making a circle of steam around her cheeks.

The paper was crisp and new, but terribly old-fashioned to Kami's way of thinking. In Gothic font, the paper read, "Moose Jaw *Evening Times.*" But it was the date which caught and held her attention. July 6, 1926. She groaned, her knees buckling beneath her as her hands hit the floor with a bang.

"Who's there?" a gruff voice rasped. Kami heard the sound of frenzied activity inside the office. She rolled to the edge of the platform and slid off and underneath it as the office door slammed open and Stanford burst out.

Footsteps stomped across the platform while Kami hid underneath. "Who's there?" Stanford called out again as he came down the three steps and moved around the platform to the side where Kami was hiding. She could see his scuffed boots tapping impatiently and figured he was searching the area, trying to decide where the noise had come from.

"Relax," a voice called from the doorway. "It's only me."

The biggest man Kami had ever seen bent down and came through the doorway. As he neared the platform, his body was lost to her. Only his knees and below were visible.

"Oh, Mr. Maxwell. I thought I heard something out here. These darn coolies are always causing trouble. Is there a problem?"

"I'm just checking on one of my many investments, Stanford. I'm making sure you're doing your job." His voice sounded menacing and Kami shivered, hoping she wouldn't be discovered. "At least we don't get too many runners. Most just want to stay and make their money so they can bring their families here from China. Isn't it too bad it takes 'em so long?" He laughed. "I heard they raised the Head Tax again; too bad they have to pay me first. Those coolies'll be working for years before they save enough money!"

A chill ran down Kami's spine as she realized what they were talking about. This man was transporting illegal immigrants and making them work for him, and she was caught in it. She was an indentured servant, working for her freedom in underground Moose Jaw!

The men moved away from the platform and toward the doorway. Kami watched for her chance to slip away unnoticed and back to the safety of her bed. She had no choice. For now, she would stay put, watching for an opportunity to escape. In the meantime, though, she would try to fit in and not draw attention to herself. That seemed to be her best bet for survival down here.

Making it back to her bunk undetected, Kami quickly climbed up and lay down. She fell into a deep, dreamless sleep of exhaustion that ended far too soon. Within minutes, it seemed, someone was banging on the side of her bed, shaking it and angrily yelling at her in Chinese. She could almost make out the words her grandmother used to scold her with when she was stubborn and refused to do what she said. Sitting up, she waved quickly at the voice below her and then pushed the hair back from her face and climbed carefully out of bed.

Once safely on the floor, Kami tried to fix her hair. It was a mess of tangles and knots. Grandma was the one who braided it each morning, and suddenly Kami missed her terribly. Tears filled her eyes, spilling down her cheeks before she knew what was happening. She stood sobbing into her hands, wondering how she would ever cope with living down here.

Kami felt a soft touch on her shoulder. She took her hands away from her face, scrubbing at her wet cheeks, and looked up into the face of a young girl. "I can't do my hair," Kami sobbed, waving a handful of hair. The girl seemed to understand, for she sat Kami down on the edge of the lowest bed and stood behind her.

Comforting words murmured in Kami's ear as the girl swiftly rebraided her hair. She closed her eyes as the girl worked, enjoying the feeling. It felt just like Grandma was doing it and somehow it made Kami feel safer.

It was no easy task to braid the hair without a brush, but the girl managed to do a good job of it. The long, thick braid was tidy and tight and would keep the hair out of her face. It made her look like the other workers who filed toward the tables for breakfast and Kami felt much better.

"Thank you," Kami whispered, her voice still thick with tears.

The girl smiled, giving her a quick hug and then asking her a question, her dark eyes warm and friendly. She wants to know my name, Kami realized. "Kami," she told her.

"Ming," the girl said, pointing a finger at her own chest. She waved at Kami and then disappeared down the hallway.

Jimmy waved at Kami as she approached the kitchen area, saving her a place beside him. Kami desperately wanted to wash her hands and face. She gestured to Jimmy, mimicking the washing of her face. He pointed, directing her to two washbasins that stood in the far corner of the kitchen, almost out of sight. With a sigh of relief, she hurried toward them.

A greyish bit of cloth hung from a nail pounded into the wall. Kami splashed water on her face and used her hands to scrub her cheeks. Cupping water in her hands, she washed her neck. It felt good to have cool water trickling over her and made her wish she was at home taking a nice hot shower. She searched the cloth for a clean corner and patted herself dry. That was as clean as she was going to get.

In the rectangular open area between the kitchen area and the laundry machines, a group of workers stood. Kami watched, fascinated, as one of them stepped up in front of the others, who all bowed to him. He led them through a series of silent, graceful movements, a little like ballet, a little like martial arts done very slowly. What was going on? She continued to watch, remembering a group of people who met in Crescent Park every morning to do similar exercises. Whatever it was, they took it very seriously.

Kami's eyes were drawn to a girl about her own age who stepped gracefully into the pose and held it, a calm look on her face. It was Ming, she realized happily. Kami studied her closely as she held the position.

Ming was slightly taller than Kami, her arms long and graceful. How could she look so peaceful, living in these awful conditions? As they changed poses again, Ming glanced in Kami's direction and their eyes met. She smiled warmly at Kami, her dark eyes shining as she gestured for her to join them, but Kami shook her head. She was too shy right now; maybe she'd try it another time.

A clanging sound called them to breakfast and Kami went eagerly, trying to escape her thoughts. She was hungry. After that meagre dinner the night before, her stomach was rumbling. Sitting down beside Jimmy, she picked up her bowl, which he had already filled. It was steaming, full of the same thin grey soup. Bowls heaped with rice were on the table as well. Did they eat the same thing everyday? She longed for fresh bread smeared with butter, or a juicy orange.

For the first time Kami began to wonder, would she ever get home again? What if she had to live here forever? It was a sobering thought and she blinked back tears as she picked up her soup bowl, forcing herself to drink. She had to keep up her strength. After all, she was waiting for a chance to escape. It could happen any time. But what about Eddie? she wondered tearfully. Where was he? She hoped he was okay. Just let us find each other soon, please, she begged. She just wanted to go home.

THE STRANGER

"You can stay at Rosie's," Vance announced, leading the way back across the park.

"She's not home," Beanie reminded him. "She's in Regina, remember?"

"It doesn't matter," Vance continued marching through the park. "I know where she hides a key for her place. She asked me to look in on it once or twice, just to make sure everything's all right. She won't mind you using it."

By this point Andrea didn't care where they slept. She was dead on her feet. Zombie-like, she followed Vance out of the park, past the Hazelton Hotel, its lights shining out into the night, and back across Main Street. They turned onto Ominica Street with Andrea and Tony both almost asleep on their feet.

Vance led the way, their feet shuffling quietly as they walked past the darkened windows of Rosie's neighbours. At the house he paraded them up the front walk and onto the porch. The front door squeaked slightly as they pulled it open. Motioning for them to be quiet, he tiptoed up the stairs to Rosie's suite. Once there, he fumbled with the skeleton key he found on the ledge above the door. Turning the key, he pushed the door open. "There you go! Home sweet home!"

Relief flooded Andrea's exhausted limbs as she stumbled into the kitchen. Everything looked exactly the same. The kitchen table was still under the window in the corner of the room, the wooden chairs placed neatly around it. The two doors leading into the small bedrooms were tightly shut. "Are you sure Rosie won't mind?"

Beanie gave her a reassuring pat on the arm. "You know Rosie, she'd be mad if you didn't make yourself at home here." She rummaged around in the cupboards. "Looks like she left some food around. How odd, since she knew she was leaving. Oh well, eat whatever you want. Rosie won't mind at bit."

Andrea glanced at Tony. "How are you doing? We'd better get you something to eat to keep your blood-sugar levels up."

Nodding sleepily, Tony pulled off his backpack. "I have a peanut butter sandwich in my bag, and a juice box. I told you I was prepared." Pulling out his sandwich and juice, he sat down at the table and began to eat.

"I'm sorry to seem rushed," Vance said, heading toward the door. "I have to get up early to sell newspapers, and I'm beat." He pushed away from the door. "Come on, Beanie, let's get home. We'll see you two tomorrow."

Tony had already finished the sandwich. He headed into the spare bedroom and dropped his backpack on the floor with a thump. Pulling off his shoes he fell into bed. "'Night," he muttered. He was asleep before his head hit the pillow. Andrea sighed, leaning against the doorframe as she watched her brother sleep for a moment. She was glad he only needed his insulin shot once a day and he took it in the morning, so he didn't need to bother with it now.

Andrea glanced around the room. It looked different somehow, but she was too tired to do more than lean there, trying to get up enough energy to go to bed. Whatever it was, the tiny room seemed more crowded than ever.

"Who's there?" a soft voice called out. Andrea jumped, stifling a scream. Her elbow knocked against the door, sending it crashing against the wall with a loud bang. Spiky tingles of pain raced up and down her arm as she stared at the image. A ghost-like figure in shimmering white stood just inside Rosie's bedroom door.

"Who are you?" Andrea and the apparition demanded at once. They stood glaring at one another across the room and Andrea realized with relief that at least the figure was human. It was a slight girl just a few years older than she was.

The kitchen door sprang open again as Vance and Beanie burst into the door. "What's going on?" Vance demanded, his hands on his hips. His eyes fell on the stranger. "Who are you, and what are you doing in Rosie's apartment?"

The girl stubbornly stood her ground, although Andrea could see her fingers trembling as she balled them into fists. She stood glaring at Vance, her hands on her hips. "What right do you have barging in here like this at this time of night? Get out before I scream! The police will get here on the double!"

Grabbing at Vance's arm, Beanie tried to pull him back toward the entrance. "Come on, Vance. Let's go. We don't want any trouble."

Shaking her off like a pesky fly, Vance stalked toward the girl. "Who are you and what are you doing in Rosie's apartment?" he repeated, coming within a hair's breadth of her, his hands on his hips. He was a head and shoulders taller, but she refused to back down. "Rosie never made mention of anyone staying here. I think we have an intruder on our hands. Beanie, go get the police now!"

"Yes," the girl agreed. "Go get the police. You'll see

that I have every right to be here." She stalked across the room, putting distance between herself and Vance. "I'm not leaving until the police come and arrest you for breaking in!"

"What?" Vance exclaimed, "We're not here to steal anything. We're just looking for a place for our – uh – our friends, I mean, relatives, to spend the night."

"Ah-ha!" the girl exclaimed as she flounced past Vance, her nightgown swirling around her bare feet. "A likely story! You're fibbing! I only see one person, where's the other?"

Right on cue, Tony pushed the bedroom door open and stood in the doorway. He yawned widely. "What's all the racket? Can't a guy get any sleep around here?"

The girl gave a screech of fear and practically threw Tony out of the way. "Get out of there! You keep away from him!" She stood just inside the bedroom barring the way, her arms stretched wide. "All of you get out of here now!"

"Away from whom?" Andrea asked, but she already knew the answer. She heard the distinctive sound of baby talk and the unsteady patter of small feet just learning to walk. The girl's nightgown waved and flared to one side and Baby Alan tottered out into the kitchen. Silently he studied each person, his lower lip trembling.

"Leave him alone!" the girl ordered, reaching to

grab the baby, but it was too late.

"Ban! Ban!" Baby Alan chortled. Raising his hands, he raced on unsteady legs across the floor and flung himself into Vance's outstretched arms.

"Hiya, Sprout," Vance grinned, lifting Baby Alan high over his head and swinging him around. The baby laughed gleefully as he came down to rest on Vance's shoulder. "Where's your ma? I thought I heard some of the newspaper guys saying you were going to Regina with her."

Everyone stood staring at one another in the silent kitchen. Even the baby seemed to feel the tension. He grabbed a handful of Vance's hair with one hand and stuck the thumb of his other hand in his mouth, leaning his cheek against the top of Vance's head.

"Well," the girl finally said, sounding breathless and unsure. "If you're a friend of Alan's, you must be a friend of Rosie's…" She trailed off, seeming to realize for the first time that she was standing and talking to strangers in her nightgown! "I don't usually entertain dressed like this," she said, smoothing her hands over the thick flannel material. "But then, most company doesn't usually arrive after midnight! Was that you banging on the door a while ago? You scared the life out of me! Rosie told me not to open the door so late, so I didn't, and now you're back!"

"Who are you?" Vance asked again, trying unsuccessfully to untangle his hair from Baby Alan's fingers.

"I'm Sarah, a friend of Rosie's. I just got into town a week ago. I'm looking for work, or I was. It happened that Rosie had just gotten the offer to go to Regina and I appeared on her doorstep. So, I'm here taking care of Baby Alan and Rosie is in Regina. It's easier for her that way, and it gives me a place to stay too." She eyed the others, darts of suspicion shooting across the room.

Andrea decided to make the first move. "I'm Andrea." She reached up and held her arms out to Baby Alan. He stared at her for a moment and then smiled, a four-toothed grin that melted her heart. Releasing his hold on Vance's hair, he slid off Vance's shoulder, plopping himself neatly into Andrea's waiting arms. "Hi," she cooed, brushing her lips against his soft cheek. "Remember me?"

"What about me?" Tony asked, reaching up to rub Baby Alan's head. His hair was light brown, thin and straight, not unlike Andrea's when it was short. "Do you remember your old pal Tony? I'll bet you'd like this!" He reached for his juice box on the table. "Here, have a sip."

"What is that?" Sarah asked as Tony helped the baby put the straw in his mouth.

Andrea and Vance exchanged swift, knowing gazes across the room, and in the silence of the kitchen, a decision was made. In the quick voiceless conference, the two oldest participants, Vance and Andrea, had decided not to tell Sarah their huge secret. After all,

Andrea thought, the fewer people who knew about the time travel adventures, the better.

"It's just —" Beanie stumbled over the words. "It's like — magic."

Sarah grabbed the juice box away from Baby Alan and inspected it closely, turning it in her hands. "I've never seen anything like this before in my life." A few drops of juice spilled into the palm of her hand. Poking her finger into the droplets of juice, she sniffed at it. "Orange juice," she announced. Sticking her tongue out, she hesitantly licked her finger, then nodded. "Why put juice in these funny little boxes? That doesn't make sense."

"Not a lot about us will make sense, Sarah," Andrea stated, her voice comforting. She could only imagine how confused and doubtful she must be feeling, staring at Andrea and Tony with so many unanswered questions bombarding her mind. "We're — uh-h-h, we're relatives of Vance and Beanie; travelers from — um, far away," she finished lamely, wondering if Sarah believed her. It sounded so phony.

"These two really do need a place to stay," Vance said, his voice pleading.

Sarah's lips pursed together in a frown. "I don't know —" Her gaze swept past Vance and fell on Andrea and Tony, her eyes narrowing as she studied them.

Andrea now understood what was meant when

someone said, "The tension in the room was so thick you could cut it with a knife." It felt heavy and awkward, as if they were all waiting for something to happen. Vance stood frozen near the doorway, clutching his cap tightly between his fingers. Beanie watched nearby, twisting a lock of dirty blonde hair around one finger.

"They really are friends of Rosie's," Beanie said, her voice sincere. "They need a place to stay. They're not dangerous criminals, you know."

"What did you say your names were?" Sarah asked, her eyes mistrusting.

"Andrea and Tony Talbot," Andrea replied gently. She could understand why Sarah was apprehensive.

"Talbot?" Sarah questioned. "Rosie talked about having friends with that last name. Viola, I think, was one name she mentioned, but I think her name is Paterson now. Didn't she get married recently?"

"Viola's our great-grandm —" Andrea dug her elbow into Tony's ribs to silence him.

"She's our ma," Beanie quickly added trying to cover Tony's blunder. She didn't want Sarah asking too many questions.

"I guess you can stay," Sarah said reluctantly. "I hope it'll be all right with Rosie."

Tony sighed, a huge sound that nearly filled the room. "I'm so glad. It's almost like coming back to my second home. I always feel safe here, Grandpa."

"Time to go," Vance cut in quickly, his eyes darting to Sarah and then away. Grabbing Beanie's arm, he herded her toward the door.

Sarah followed them, intent on being a good hostess, even in her nightgown.

"Thank you for letting them stay," Vance said, folding and unfolding the brim of his cap in his hands. He looked so awkward that Andrea felt sorry for him. He wasn't usually this way with people, even strangers. "I'm Vance, by the way," he said, offering Sarah his large hand.

After the briefest moment, Sarah put her hand in his and smiled. "I'm Sarah."

"I'm Beanie." She pulled on Sarah's sleeve, trying to get her attention, but Sarah only had eyes for Vance.

"Well, Beanie," Vance slapped his cap on his head. "Let's let Sarah get our friends to bed. It's awfully late and I'm beat."

"I'll come by tomorrow," Beanie told Andrea, blowing a kiss in Baby Alan's direction. He sat perched on Andrea's arm, his head nestling in her shoulder.

"Wave bye-bye," Sarah said, opening and closing her hand at Beanie and Vance. Alan blinked a few times then took his thumb out of his mouth. Small fingers bent once and then stood up soldier straight. The sound of cheers and clapping caught his attention and he looked around, waving again. "Show-off," Sarah smiled, taking him and kissing his neck. "It's nighty-night for you." She put him back to bed quickly and then came out into the kitchen again, hovering near the doorway.

Andrea hid a yawn behind her hand. "I'm ready for bed too."

"Me too," Tony replied. "Can I sleep in there again?" He pointed to Rosie's spare bedroom.

Sarah nodded, her eyes studying Andrea. "Come on," she said reluctantly. "You might as well sleep with me. It's a big bed – I guess I'll be safe enough."

Meekly, pleased that she wouldn't have to share that tiny bed with Tony again, like she'd had to last year, Andrea followed Sarah into the bedroom. "Thank you, Sarah, you're being very generous, under the circumstances."

Sarah grunted. She pulled open a drawer and tossed a garment on the bed between them. "Here, wear this, you'll be more comfortable. I don't even want to know why you're dressed in that ridiculous outfit. You look like a boy!" Crawling under the covers, she turned her back on Andrea and pretended to sleep.

Gratefully, Andrea blinked tears from her eyes and held her tongue. How could she explain about time travel and needing to wear a disguise in the tunnels? It would be like fairy stories to Sarah, fun to listen to, but not true. As Andrea prepared for bed, she knew she'd have to find some way to thank Sarah for being so generous and trusting of strangers. Andrea wasn't sure she would have been as gracious in the same situation.

EDDIE LEARNS THE ROPES

E ddie counted himself lucky. He'd gotten off easy, with only a few bruises on his back and shoulders from Mean-Eyed Max and the man with the rod. His shoulders ached, but at least he could still work. He wondered, though, what would have happened if the sound of sirens hadn't been heard in the distance.

"Get everyone inside quickly!" Mean-Eyed Max had commanded as the sound got louder, forgetting about Eddie.

Back in the basement, Eddie had heard the other man say, "The cops are on our tails these days. We can't be too careful. We'd better hide these workers."

They had dragged Eddie into the basement room and across the floor. Gesturing and yelling at him, they had made it clear that they wanted him to work, opening the crates. When the other man had started to explain how to open the cases, Mean-Eyed Max stopped him. "Don't waste your breath," he'd said, pointing at all the workers. "They don't speak English, remember?"

"It's a good thing," the other man had replied. "Let's hope it stays that way."

Shoving Eddie toward the stack of unopened cases, Mean-Eyed Max had shown him how to take off the tops, using a crowbar for leverage. "Check the fruit," he said, feeling around in the sawdust to find the pro-duce. "Pull out only the most rotten ones," he showed Eddie, shoving a rotten apple into his face and then tossing it into a nearby pail. "The rest can be sold upstairs." He left Eddie searching with both hands through the sawdust, finding apples and squeezing them to test for firmness.

His hands shaking from shock, Eddie tried to catch his breath and calm his beating heart. What was going on? What did those men mean when they said no one spoke English? He peered up, covertly watching the others work. The risk of a police raid now gone, they had been ordered to continue with their duties. They trudged silently up and down the stairs, slowly and steadily like the tiny ants he had studied on the side-walk in the summer. No one talked or laughed; they just bent their heads and worked.

Nearby another boy was opening cases too. The wood creaked as it sprang open and he looked up, grinning when he realized he was being watched. He nodded at Eddie and spoke a few words softly.

"Pardon?" Eddie said, but he knew he had heard correctly. The boy was speaking Chinese! Although he knew some of the language, Eddie had always tried not to speak it, much to his grandparent's disappointment. Concentrating hard, he motioned for the boy to repeat himself. The boy was trying to tell him his name. "Kenny," he said, followed by a long string of Chinese words. He was thanking Eddie for trying to come to his rescue.

Eddie nodded and pointed to himself. "Eddie," he said.

"Eddie." Kenny bowed and grinned again, looking mischievous. He looked like the kind of boy Eddie would like to be friends with. They worked side by side long into the night, opening cases of fruit, pulling out the rotten ones and closing the cases again.

Other workers came from time to time to move the checked cases across the warehouse to another table. Eddie noticed something strange going on over there. Several workers were gathered around a table putting something into small cloth sacks. These were tied tightly and then put into the cases with the good apples. Then the lids of the crates were nailed back on again. Were they smuggling something? He tried not to stare, especially with Mean-Eyed Max walking back and forth around the area. Whatever was going on, he was sure it was illegal.

Even though they didn't speak the same language, Eddie and Kenny managed to communicate through gestures and slow enunciation. Many times Eddie mentally kicked himself for not taking his Chinese language more seriously. Now he wished he had studied harder and used it more.

Kenny, meanwhile, seemed thrilled to realize that Eddie spoke English, and whenever no one was within earshot, he would point at something and demand the English name. It became a game for them, pointing out an object and telling each other the name in their own tongue. It was a way to pass the long evening and a way to forge a new friendship.

By the end of the shift, Eddie was sore, tired, and smelled like a compost heap. He followed Kenny down a winding, narrow tunnel a short distance to a cramped room, which held decrepit looking bunk beds. Did they expect him to sleep on one of those?

Eddie watched as Kenny pointed to a vacant bed. Standing still for a moment, he realized he was tired to the bone. Not bothering to remove his shoes, he fell into the lower bunk Kenny pointed out to him. A pillow of sorts, made out of a burlap sack with some of the sawdust for stuffing, cushioned his head. A thin, ragged pieced of material was his blanket, while a lumpy, straw-filled mattress substituted for his bed. He collapsed onto it and was asleep within a few seconds.

The smell of cooking and many voices calling back and forth drifted into his consciousness and pulled Eddie out of a deep, dreamless sleep. "Where am I?" he questioned, raising his head to look around. His forehead hit the upper bunk and he winced, remembering. The clatter of dishes on wood caught his attention and he followed the sound with his eyes. Several Chinese workers sat at long tables, obviously waiting to eat. Some worked quietly, writing with what looked like paintbrushes. Most talked quietly among themselves.

A sense of dread filled Eddie's stomach as he surveyed the scene before him. He had hoped that he'd been dreaming and that he would wake up at home in his nice soft bed with his computer sitting across the room. Pictures and words flashed through his brain as he broke out in a cold sweat. Was this real life?

Pinching himself hard, Eddie looked around, waiting for things to go back to normal. Nothing changed. The view before him remained old-fashioned, rustic, and permanent. Despair settled in the pit of his stomach like an unwelcome houseguest and he wondered what would become of him.

Kenny approached the bed, his hands hidden

behind his back. He talked excitedly, his voice rising and falling rapidly. The other workers began to crowd around the bed too. What did they want?

With a flourish, Kenny dropped a newspaper into Eddie's lap and gestured for him to read it. Picking it up, Eddie stared at the headlines and felt the bottom drop out of his world. He was holding a brand new copy of the Moose Jaw *Evening Times*. The year read 1926. Here was proof. He was an indentured servant, caught back in time in the tunnels of Moose Jaw!

Somehow, his head whirling, Eddie managed to read and translate part of the news to the other workers, although he couldn't remember a word of it. Thanking him with bows of gratitude, the others slowly drifted away, leaving Eddie alone. He lay back on the bunk and shut his eyes, pretending to sleep, desperately needing time to try to figure things out. Where was Kami? Was she all right? What about Andrea and Tony? Had they been pulled back in time too?

Eddie must have dozed off again, for the next thing he knew, Kenny was shaking him awake, gesturing for him to come and eat. Feeling light-headed and still very confused, he allowed himself to be led over to the kitchen area. The food was meagre at best. A thin greyish looking soup and bowls of rice and endless pots of tea were served. Hungry, he ate, although he longed for something more substantial. No wonder these workers were so thin and tired. They weren't getting enough to eat and not much protein either, as far as Eddie could see.

Why did these people stay here? The question floated around Eddie's brain as he sat among them. They seemed resigned to this life, almost happy in some ways, while all he thought about was trying to find a way to escape. Thinking hard, Eddie finally managed to find the right Chinese words and awkwardly phrased the question to Kenny.

Looking surprised, Kenny spoke rapidly and Eddie could barely understand.

"Slowly," Eddie begged, and he watched Kenny's lips as he formed the words. Painfully, the story began to unfold. Kenny's parents had managed to save up enough money to pay his passage to Canada. They hadn't known about the tax on Chinese people, but even if they had, they wouldn't have been able to afford it, and Kenny didn't have the heart to tell them about it. So he worked here in the tunnels, trying to pay his Head Tax and save enough money to send back to China for his family. It was his great hope to someday bring his mother and father and little brother to live here. That was why the men worked here in the tunnels.

"All of these people?" Eddie asked, pointing at them. Kenny nodded. "They have to pay a tax to live in Canada?"

Kenny nodded. "A Head Tax."

"How much do you get paid to work here?" Eddie asked. Kenny dug into his pocket and pulled out a twenty-five-cent piece, proudly showing it to him. "A day?!" Eddie was sure he'd misunderstood, but Kenny nodded.

Eddie thought of all the hard work these people were doing. They deserved way more than that, even if it was 1926. How could you save anything when you only made a quarter a day? Still, they had hope, and a job, even though it wasn't a great one.

First they had to save money to pay the Head Tax, and then they had to save money to bring their families to Canada. Basically, they were as good as slaves until they had saved enough money to pay off the tax and live legally in Canada. No wonder they stayed. No one was eager to escape but him. He watched as they went off to work, reluctantly joining them. He knew it would be a long, tedious day.

After work, Eddie went back to his bunk and lay down, the muscles in his arms sore. He was exhausted, and he wondered if he would be able to survive the long hours and hard work. He needed to get out of here. A plan began to hatch in his mind. He would go out the door they had brought him in through and escape down that tunnel. He had to go back that way, because Kami was down here somewhere too. He hoped she wasn't caught up in something like this. It would be terrible for her and she would be very frightened. His sister could be a pest at times, he admitted, but he loved her and he didn't want her to be in any pain. On that thought, he fell into a deep sleep.

Eddie woke up with a start some time later. Loud snores filled the room and someone grunted. That must have been what had woken him up. He lay still, wondering why he hadn't seen or heard the man with the rod or the other guard. They obviously weren't very good at the job of guarding people. Or maybe they were just sure that no one wanted to escape.

This would be so simple, Eddie thought with a grin. He'd just sneak out of the door and into the tunnel and be gone.

Slipping from the bed, Eddie tiptoed through the narrow tunnel and then across the floor. He carefully weaved his way around the cases of fruit stacked nearby. Knocking into one of those piles would be disastrous.

It was dark except for a small light near the entrance. Keeping his eyes peeled on that light, Eddie cautiously made his way toward the door. He smiled to himself. Soon he would be free.

Reaching the door, Eddie carefully pulled it open. It creaked slightly, but he was confident no one had heard the sound. The blackness of the tunnel greeted him and he almost turned back. It was scary, and he didn't like the idea of travelling through it without any light. What if he got lost? What if he couldn't find his way out?

Bravely pushing these thoughts away, Eddie stepped out into the tunnel, dragging the door closed. It was stuck. He pulled harder, but nothing happened. Grabbing the edge of the door with both hands he tried in vain to pull it shut. Something was in the way. What was that object on the floor blocking the door? In the darkness it was difficult to tell. Bending, Eddie grasped it and tried to push it out of the way. Bits of cotton string caught in his fingers as he pushed, his hand encountering soft leather.

"Going somewhere, coolie?"

ANDREA'S DRASTIC DECISION

"Let's concentrate on getting to the girl first," Vance said between large bites of bread. In true Vance style, once he'd made up his mind to help, he was in on the job one hundred percent. "At least we know where she is."

They all sat around Rosie's wooden table eating bread and fruit. Glancing around at the faces, Andrea missed Rosie acutely. She wished Rosie were here to advise them. They could sure use her help and practical suggestions right now.

Sarah had reluctantly prepared breakfast, refusing to let them help with anything. Barely speaking a word to anyone, she darted suspicious looks toward Andrea and Tony several times, her lips pinched in a thin, disapproving line. Good thing she hadn't seen

Tony give himself his insulin shot this morning, Andrea thought with a grin. Then she'd really have something to be suspicious about!

"I'm taking Baby Alan for a walk," Sarah announced, coming out of the bedroom with Alan on her arm. She looked undecided, as if she should stay and watch over Rosie's house.

"You go right ahead," Vance said gallantly, jumping up eagerly to open the door for her. "See you two later."

Looking over her shoulder, Sarah stood for a moment wondering what to do. Then, shrugging, she turned and marched down the stairs, Baby Alan waving bye-bye at them as they left.

"He's so cute," Andrea cooed, blowing a kiss his way.

"I'm glad she's gone," Tony said, finishing his breakfast. "It feels funny around here with her always staring at us."

"This gives us the chance to talk openly," Vance said, turning back slowly toward the table. "Let's get back to this rescue operation."

"They might have just taken Kami through the warehouse and out the other end. We don't know if she's still there," Beanie pointed out as she reached for another piece of bread.

"Beanie's right," Andrea agreed, trying to convince herself to eat. Her stomach was still doing panicky somersaults and she was worried that she might be sick. "We'll have to get into the warehouse somehow without being seen and try to find her."

"That's impossible," Vance said flatly, his spoon banging on the table with finality.

"It would be dangerous," Andrea agreed. "We'd probably be spotted, sneaking around. I think that, wherever they keep these workers, they're always watching them to make sure they don't escape. It wouldn't work at all, trying to get into the warehouse unnoticed."

"Is that what it's like down there?" Beanie questioned, shuddering. "It sounds pretty scary and miserable for those poor people."

Vance snorted. "I still don't believe there are workers underground. Where are they? I've been in all the tunnels! I've never seen Chinese people down there, servants or otherwise. I think Mean-Eyed Max took your friends for another reason and is holding them captive. But either way," he sighed, running his fingers through his hair in an anxious gesture that left it tousled and untidy, "we do have to rescue them. Any ideas of how we can do it?"

They finished their meal slowly, each thinking up and discarding plans, calling out: "What if we —" and "How about —" but every idea was too risky, too silly, too dangerous. It looked as if nothing would work.

"What if we could find a legitimate way to get into the warehouse?" Andrea asked.

115

"Like what?" Vance replied, pushing his empty bowl across the table.

"Like – like – delivering something to them –" Andrea continued, thinking so hard her brain felt as if it was sweating.

"Or we could get hired by them – you know, work for the bad guys like you did before!" Tony piped up. He was so excited about the prospect that he squirmed from side to side in his seat, rocking the chair back and forth on two legs as he moved.

"I bet I could get hired as a tunnel rat!" Andrea exclaimed.

"No, not you," Vance decided, darting an appraising look in her direction.

"Why not me?" Andrea asked, her voice angry. "I've been a tunnel runner before and I was darned good at it too!"

"One of the best," Vance agreed. "After all, I taught you everything you know, and you did rescue me. But Andrea," he said, looking her up and down, his acute embarrassment evident. His face grew red and he ducked his head, studiously searching the floor. "You've grown up, you know. You look too much like a girl, even in those overalls. They only hire fellas to do tunnel work. That's why you disguised yourself as a boy in the first place, remember?"

"I'll do it then," Tony shouted, jumping from his seat. "I'll be a tunnel rat and save Kami."

"It'd be too dangerous for you," Vance said.

"But you can't do it by yourself," Beanie said. "Really, two of us should be going in together to look for jobs. I could —"

"No!" Vance said, blue eyes pinched in determination. "You're not going into those tunnels again, Beanie. I promised our stepdad I'd keep you safe, and I mean to do just that."

Everyone looked pensively around the room, hoping an idea or inspiration would jump out of a corner and save the day, but none did. Silence fell as they sat at the table. A lazy fly buzzed past the open window, sounding like the drone of a biplane in the quiet kitchen.

After several minutes of heavy sighing, Andrea reached up and pulled the rest of her hair from its messy ponytail. Shaking it free, she finger-combed it, letting it fall in yellow disarray around her shoulders. "I guess there's no other way," she announced, standing and moving her chair to the center of the crowded kitchen.

She began to pace the room, her mind made up. "We need another boy and we don't have one. A disguise won't work because I look too much like a girl. But what if I borrow some of Vance's clothes; a big baggy shirt and bigger overalls?" Voices began to murmur in disagreement, but Andrea waved them silent. "Hear me out. I do have an idea. What if —" she cringed and began pacing again, gathering courage.

Squaring her shoulders, Andrea plunked herself down into her chair. "Get the scissors, Beanie," she ordered resolutely. "You're going to cut my hair."

Beanie lifted the heavy ceramic bowl off Andrea's head with a flourish. "There," she announced. "You're all done!"

Blinking from the bright light suddenly hitting her eyes, Andrea shook her head. She was surprised that people actually used bowls to cut hair! How silly, how archaic. Then she remembered, she was back in the 1920s, after all.

Tufts of dirty blonde hair littered the wooden floor around Andrea's chair. "Well?" she whispered to the stunned group, her own face pale, large brown eyes intent. "How do I look?" Eyes scattered like seeds on the wind to the furthest corners of the room. "Is it that bad?" Unshed tears made her eyes luminous. "How bad is it?"

"Well, no girl would have hair like that in our time, that's for sure, but it's not as bad as that short spiky do you had the first time I met you," Vance asserted, shaking his head as if he didn't quite understand Andrea or the modern ways.

"It's fine," Beanie asserted in a quivery voice that could have belonged to Aunt Bea. Clearing her throat, she tried again. "You look like – like –"

"Like a boy," Tony finished bluntly, staring at his sister.

"Well," Andrea said, brown eyes solemn, her voice shaking with emotion, "that *is* what I wanted – I think..."

Vance circled her like a lynx eyeing its prey. "You look just like me," he declared, "when I was a few years younger."

"Except for the eyes," Beanie added. "Andrea has beautiful brown eyes." She smiled in Andrea's direction. "That haircut draws attention to your eyes."

Andrea smiled, a ghost of a smile that quickly faded from her lips. "Thanks, Beanie," she sighed, almost regretting her rash decision. Oh well, what was done was done, and she'd have to live with it now. She'd worry about the consequences later. Right now she and Vance had a job to do. If the haircut would help her rescue Kami and Eddie, then she'd done the right thing. That was the important part to remember. Boy, would she ever have stories to tell her children and grandchildren!

"I'm going to go change into Vance's clothes," Andrea announced, indicating the large pair of overalls and baggy flannel shirt Vance had sprinted home to get while she sat under the bowl. "The rest of you come up with some kind of plan. Why are we stumped with this? We've dealt with bad guys before.

I'm beginning to get really worried about Kami and Eddie. What if Mean-Eyed Max gets tired of having them around? What if they don't co-operate with the bad guys?"

No one had answers, and the dismal silence deepened as Andrea slipped like a shadow out of the kitchen. Stepping into the spare bedroom, she softly closed the door behind her, expelling a huge gush of air from her lungs. A small mirror hung on the wall over the dresser and curiosity got the best of her. Standing on tiptoe, she peered into the mirror. Large sorrowful eyes gazed back. She hated the new haircut on sight. Rounded in the shape of the bowl Beanie had placed on her head, the cut looked blunt and unfinished. "You'd better appreciate this, Kami," she muttered through clenched teeth.

"You look more like a boy all the time," Tony said, tossing Andrea's cap toward her as she came back into the kitchen area wearing Vance's clothes. "This will help too."

There was a sudden noise at the door and they froze as Sarah rattled the knob and then pushed the door open. "In you go," she said to Baby Alan as she set him down on the floor. He teetered toward Vance as Sarah closed the door behind her.

Looking up, Sarah took in the scene spread out before her. It was like walking on stage in the middle of a play, the actors frozen in character. A chair stood in the centre of the room, wisps of dirty blonde hair scattered like dandelion fluff on the floor around it. Beanie held the broom ready to clean up the mess. Tony sat at the table, his hands in his knapsack. Vance stood looking at Andrea, whose hands reached to place the hat on her head.

"What's going on?" Sarah demanded, her hands on her hips. "You all look so guilty! Are you planning to rob a bank?" She looked ready to grab Alan and flee.

"No," Vance tried to reassure her, "of course we're not."

"Why did you cut your hair?" Sarah persisted, staring at Andrea as if she'd suddenly grown three heads.

"You wouldn't believe us if we told you." Andrea finished pulling the soft brim hat onto her head, wondering what they could say to Sarah that would alleviate her fears but give nothing away.

Vance, taking the coward's way out, ignored Sarah. He brushed by her to do a cursory inspection of Andrea. "You'll do," he pronounced, slapping her on the back.

"So what's the plan?" Andrea wanted to know.

"We'll wait until evening," Vance said, glancing out the kitchen window. "That old warehouse'll soon be a hive of activity. We'll just saunter down to the corner and see if they can use a couple of extra fellas to help with the work. What do you think?"

Shrugging her shoulders, Andrea said, "Well, it's as

good a plan as any, and I sure don't have one right now. I just hope we can get into that warehouse. What kind of work do they do there, anyway?"

"It was a furniture factory last year. Remember when we had to rescue you? There was furniture piled everywhere," Beanie announced proudly. "Now they have a laundry business going on. The storefront faces Main Street. That's the kind of job you'll probably get, delivering laundry." Andrea thought fleetingly of the police officers they had seen, and their suspicious actions. There must be more going on there than that.

Beanie seemed to be a fount of information about the warehouse. "Have you been in those tunnels again, Beatrice Talbot?" Vance thundered, towering over her, his eyes boring into hers.

"No, Vance," she replied in a not-quite-so-innocent tone that left Vance guessing.

"Never mind about where Beanie got the information," Andrea said, coming to her rescue. "Let's just concentrate on this job. Now, all of that sounds good as long as it puts us near the workers," Andrea commented. "I just want to find Kami fast and get out of there."

"I want to come too," Tony said. "I can help."

"Me too," Beanie asserted. "Give us a job, please."

"No," Vance and Andrea both said together, scowling at their siblings.

"You're staying here," Andrea informed Tony. "I

won't have you running around on the loose. I need you here. I can't be worried about you and Kami and Eddie at the same time!"

Sarah took all the information in, her head whipping from one speaker to the speaker. "Tunnels? Bad guys? What is going on?" When no one was forthcoming with information, she grabbed Baby Alan and swung him up into her arms. "I'm going to the police," she announced, turning on her heel.

"No!" they all yelled.

Vance sprinted to the door ahead of her and blocked the exit. "Please don't go to the police. We're not doing anything illegal."

Not exactly, Andrea thought. "Their dad is a policeman."

"Then why don't you tell him what's happening. I'm sure he'd help out."

Andrea wasn't so sure about that, but she kept her mouth shut.

"He would if he was here," Beanie said, "but he's away on his honeymoon with our ma, remember?"

Sarah's blue eyes darted suspiciously around the room at them. "I don't understand what's going on, but I remember Rosie talking about Constable Paterson. I won't go to the police – yet."

"Thank you," Vance breathed a huge sigh of relief, taking her hand. "We'll explain it all to you soon."

All? Andrea wondered. Would they explain everything to Sarah, even the time travel stuff?

"Well," Sarah said, taking the broom from Beanie and sweeping up the hair, "the first thing you can explain to me is why a girl wants to look and dress like a boy."

BEING A TUNNEL RAT

The air was cooling off and evening shadows lengthened over the grass as Vance and Andrea hurried down the street. She felt awkward and bulky in the clothes Vance had brought her. The legs of the overalls had been rolled up and bounced around her ankles when she walked.

The warehouse stood on the corner of Ominica Street, an immense brick building with two huge doors facing Ominica Street and one in the alley behind. "What do we do now?" Andrea asked as they neared the building.

"We wait," Vance replied, leaning against the building near the large wooden doors. "Someone will be coming sooner or later."

"I'm scared," Andrea admitted, standing beside

Vance in the shadow of the building.

"I don't blame you," Vance said slowly. Reaching down, he plucked one of the long grass stems growing up the side of the building. He clenched it between his teeth and tilted his head back to gaze at the evening sky.

"There's something really dangerous about Mean-Eyed Max," Andrea continued, shivering even though it was warm outside.

Vance leaned against the building, studying the sky. "I don't know much about him and I sure haven't heard anything about the Chinese living in the tunnels." He shook his head.

"Maybe it does make sense," he said, finally taking the time to weigh the evidence in his mind. "That's the strange part, though. You'd think that I'd know a lot, being a former tunnel rat and hanging around with the gangsters, and getting caught up in all that trouble with you the last time. And being a newspaper boy too, I should be in the know, but I'm not. No one seems to be talking about this. If there are Chinese people working in the tunnels, it's the best-kept secret in Moose Jaw."

"Maybe no one talks to you about things like this because they know your stepfather's a policeman. They probably think you'd squeal on them." Andrea sighed, feeling tears gather in her eyes. "I wish Rosie was here. She'd know what to do."

"She sure would," Vance agreed, leading the way away from the building. "So would my stepdad."

Andrea remembered the scene she and Tony had witnessed with the two policemen, right on this very spot. It was on the tip of her tongue to ask Vance if he really trusted his new stepdad, Officer Paterson. She hesitated and the moment was lost.

"Hey, Vance!" A boy about Vance's age was just crossing the street, heading toward the warehouse.

"Hi, Jack," Vance replied, moving away from the wall. "He's another newsboy," he told Andrea, "but it looks like he moonlights as a delivery boy too."

"Want a job?" Jack called out into the night.

"What?" Vance whirled around, not sure he'd heard correctly.

"I said, do you and your friend want a job for the night? I can't promise it for longer, but two of the boys just got picked up by the cops. I'm not sure what they did, but they'll be busy for the night, down at the station. We need help running the deliveries from here. Are you interested?"

Jack pulled off his soft-brim hat, ruffling his dark hair. It was cut in a similar style to Vance's and gave him a roguish appeal that Andrea found attractive, especially when he smiled. Too bad she had to pretend to be a boy with guys like Jack nearby, she thought with chagrin.

A few other boys, all dressed much the same as

Andrea and Vance in overalls and old work shirts, some faded and torn, began to gather around them.

"We might be," Vance said cautiously.

"Pay's good," Jack said. "And you'd really be saving my skin. Mean-Eyed Max gets really foul-tempered if things don't go his way."

Vance turned to Andrea, searching her eyes. "What do you think?"

Andrea almost laughed out loud with relief. It was just what they'd been hoping would happen! This opportunity was a godsend, almost a miracle. They had to take the chance. "Let's do it, Vance."

The boys gathered closer, slapping both Vance and Andrea on the back as they began to move toward the warehouse. Andrea's shoulders burned and she almost had the wind knocked out of her a couple of times from some of the more exuberant slaps.

"What's your name?" Jack asked as they neared the door. "You're new in town. I haven't seen you around before."

Andrea pulled the cap low over her eyes. "Andy," she said firmly, trying to make her voice low and gruff. A few of them looked at her for a second or two, their gazes lingering on her face. Were they already figuring out that she was a girl?

"Welcome, Andy," Jack said, oblivious to the stares Andrea was getting from some of the other boys. "This is sure to be an exciting night for you!" He turned to the door and tapped the secret knock.

The door opened almost immediately and the boys began to dash in as quickly as possible. "Come on, come on," a snarling voice rasped in Andrea's ears. Her heart thudded, threatening to beat its way out of her chest. She must be crazy.

Trying to stay in the midst of the gang, Andrea followed their lead into the gloom. When they veered right, around a stack of wooden crates, she did too. When they turned left, just past the open office door, she did as well, but not before sneaking a quick glance in. Her heart jumped into her throat when she realized that Mean-Eyed Max was standing in the doorway watching them go past. Ducking her head, she squeezed in between two of the bigger boys. Matching their wide steps, she half-ran to stay in line with them.

"Stop!" Mean-Eyed Max called out into the murky warehouse. The blood froze in Andrea's veins, as the group became petrified statues of fear. Some of the boys turned toward the office door where the huge man lounged. "What's all the hurry tonight? You'd think you had something to hide." He spoke in a deceptively soft voice as his shoulders came through the doorframe and he moved toward the group.

Instantly visions of Ol' Scarface leaped into Andrea's paralyzed brain. She remembered how dangerous and unpredictable he was whenever he used a soft voice like that. It gave her goosebumps just thinking about it. She wondered, briefly, how much of a chance she would have making a break for it right now and running for the door. Her feet almost gave her away before her brain took over.

Realizing the folly of trying to escape when there was a guard mounted at the door, she resolutely stayed with the boys. Her heart hammered wildly in her chest. She was so scared she forgot to breathe. Pulling her cap even lower over her eyes, she tried to shrink back into the shadows created by the bigger boys. She stared mutely at the dirty floor, wishing it would open up and swallow her. She heard scuffling noises and found herself staring at Mean-Eyed Max's huge boots. He was standing right in front of her!

"Ah-h," Jack cleared his throat noisily. "Don't you think we'd better get a move on, Mean – I mean, Mr. Maxwell? We have a lot of deliveries to make tonight, remember? You told us to hurry back since there was plenty to do."

The tension hung around them in a cloud so thick Andrea felt she would choke on it. When she finally managed to open her clogged throat and breathe, the air made a wheezing sound as it swept past her constricted windpipe. "Get going, then," Mean-Eyed Max finally bellowed. His boots turned sharply and disappeared from Andrea's view.

Almost sagging with relief, she wiped sweat from her forehead and allowed herself to be swept away with the group. "Didn't see any strange fellas hanging about out there, did you?" Mean-Eyed Max called over the sound of their rushing footsteps.

"No, sir," a couple of voices replied.

"We'll be sure to keep an eye out, though," another voice answered, and Andrea was sure that it was Jack again, trying to appease Mean-Eyed Max and throw him off their trail. He was a good guy, she thought, someone who could be trusted in a pinch.

At the far end of the warehouse, a small wooden door was just barely visible. One of the boys flung it open and disappeared inside. Slowly, one by one, the boys entered the door. Jack held back, gesturing toward Andrea and Vance. "The steps are very steep," he warned them. "It's almost like a ladder, and it's very dark. Take it one step at a time, and when you get down there, wait for me."

Taking her turn, Andrea entered the doorway and began her descent down a rickety and narrow set of steps, the steepest steps she had ever encountered. The darkness was almost overwhelming and she felt as if she was back in the tunnels again. That familiar claustrophobic feeling threatened to overpower her, but she fought it off. Reaching out, she could find no railing and instead braced her hands against the walls to keep from tumbling down the stairs.

The journey seemed endless, but suddenly a dim beam of light reached her eyes and Andrea realized that she had made it to the basement level. Taking a shaky breath, she prepared to exit through the door.

As Andrea pushed the door open, a horrible smell engulfed her and she choked in surprise. It burned her throat as she drew in a shallow breath, and she coughed, sneezing at the same time. Her hand flew to her mouth and nose, but the smell permeated the air, making her stomach feel queasy. Leaning weakly against the wall, she waited for Vance, willing her weak stomach to behave itself.

The foul smell hit Vance too, as soon as he drew near, and he put his hand over his mouth and nose. "You get used to it," Jack said beside them, though Andrea could see tears in his eyes as well. "It'll hit you every time you come down here, but your symptoms will get less and less."

"What is it?" Vance demanded, wiping his mouth and nose on his shirtsleeve.

"It's everything that goes on down here; the strong cleaning solutions, the cooking smells, you name it. And they can't get any air down here to clear it out." Jack straightened up. "Come on, let's just do our job quickly and get out of here. At least we can leave here and get fresh air. Those poor beggars have to live down here." As they walked through the semi-darkness, a thrumming noise grew louder and more distinct.

A wall suddenly loomed up ahead of them. Jack pointed to an almost invisible door and then pulled it open. Waving gallantly, he let Andrea and Vance through first and then stepped inside, closing the door behind him. The smell was so rank here, Andrea could feel her nostrils burn when she breathed. How could anyone stand the odour for more than a few seconds? How could anyone actually breathe down here and live to tell about it? "Here we are," Jack announced. "Welcome to the Chinese laundry."

Gazing around in amazement, Andrea tried to take everything in at once. They were in an area about one quarter the size of the entire warehouse. Standing where they were, just inside the door, they could see almost everything that was going on in the area. To the left were at least a dozen huge tubs, steam escaping from them into the already humid air. Old-fashioned washboards lay on the floor or were propped inside the tubs.

Nearby, several furnaces blazed red hot, and crudely made irons rested on racks over the flames. Ropes were strung everywhere, all of them filled with damp clothes. "It looks like I was wrong," Vance muttered, shaking his head as he watched people work. It was a beehive of activity, each person busily doing his own job. "I can't believe what I'm seeing."

Andrea stood speechless, still trying to absorb it all. Could this actually be happening? Looking around, she watched the people work, oblivious to her. It must be late at night, she thought, trying to remember what time it was, and yet these people were still hard at work.

Some of the workers stood at the huge washing tubs. As scalding water sloshed around inside they reached bare hands into the soapy solution, pulling out clothes. Some were thrown into another tub to be rinsed, Andrea guessed. Others had to be scrubbed. She watched, her mouth hanging open, as one person picked up a metal washboard and placed it against the inside of the tub. He proceeded to scrub the garment against the washboard until she was sure his knuckles must be rubbed raw.

Andrea's attention was drawn to another person who expertly ironed a man's white shirt, lifting the heavy metal iron from the hot furnace rack and placing it on the fabric. What a horribly hot and dangerous job that was, she thought, watching as he moved the iron back and forth and then whisked it back to the furnace rack. Which job was more dangerous? she wondered.

Looking past all the activity in the laundry, Andrea saw what appeared to be an eating area. Rough-hewn lumber made up several long tables. Two huge stoves had been pushed against the far wall, and a man was stirring the contents of one huge pot while three others simmered on the stoves. The people must sleep down here too, Andrea thought. Scanning the far back wall, she noticed a darkened doorway. That probably led to the sleeping area.

"Get a move on, boys, if you want to get paid tonight!" a rough voice called out above the din, and Andrea jumped. Turning slightly to her left, she saw a scruffy looking man dressed in dungarees and a plaid shirt, much like hers. He stood on a wooden platform. Behind him was a door and a large window revealing a large wooden desk on the inside. This was obviously the overseer's platform and office, elevated about a metre off the ground to allow him to see the whole area from this one vantage point.

"That's Stanford," Jack whispered to them. "Watch out for him. He's in charge down here. He's a mean old coot." He hurried them past the line of washtubs. "Come on, I'll show you the ropes."

Moving slowly, Andrea tried to get a look at each face as she passed by. Where was Kami? How could she possibly survive this horrible place? Suddenly, Andrea felt very sorry for Kami. She hadn't known what she was getting into when she'd fallen into the tunnel, and now she was a worker somewhere in a terrible place like this.

Frustrated, Andrea realized that the Chinese workers didn't look up at all as they passed by. It was as if she, Jack, and Vance didn't even exist. They weren't interested in seeing who it was, she thought. They were probably exhausted, half poisoned from the noxious smells, and frightened. They were brave too, and determined, she decided, watching as they worked, diligently doing their assigned tasks. They each had a goal – to save enough money to pay their Head Tax and then make better lives for themselves and their families. You really had to admire these people; they weren't quitters.

At the far end of the area stood a long wooden bench. Parcels, wrapped with brown paper and tied with string, were piled high. On each parcel, written in pencil, was a name and address. "Our job is to deliver these to the addresses," Jack told them, picking up several packages. "Just leave 'em on the porch. It's late now, but we promise next-day service, and the men, especially, want their crisp, white shirts for the morning." He frowned, looking up and down the table.

"The other boys must've grabbed more than their fair share," he said, noting that only eight parcels remained. "These are mine," he said, grabbing a stubby pencil and scribbling his initials onto four of them. "Sorry, fellas, but there's only two each left for you. That's the way it works down here. Better luck next time."

Vance and Andrea shrugged their shoulders, knowing that they weren't there for a job anyway; they had to find Kami. Grabbing the remaining parcels, they followed Jack back the way they had come. As they neared the exit, he turned back, half saluting Stanford, who was carefully watching their every move.

With the din of the machines, Jack talked loudly, confident that he wouldn't be overheard. "You know, Stanford hates having to pay us boys to do this work; says we charge too much. If he could find some way to get his Chinese workers to do it, he would, but they don't speak English, and they're all in Canada illegally." Jack shrugged his shoulders, a big grin on his face. "I guess he's stuck with us!"

Jack went first this time, easily scaling the rickety steps. Andrea went next, even more cautious than before. Her hands were full of packages and there was nothing for her to hang on to if she started to fall. That thought scared her, and she moved slowly, making sure each foot was securely on the next step before moving the other. Heaving a sigh of relief, she came to the top and moved through the door and into the warehouse area. The air was fresher here, but she couldn't wait to get outside. Her lungs felt as if they were saturated with poisonous gases.

Vance right behind her, the three hurried across the warehouse floor. Andrea noticed that Mean-Eyed Max wasn't in the office. She sure didn't want to have another run-in with him. Jack reached the outside door first and pushed against it. It opened smoothly and the three stepped out into the night, breathing deeply.

"Ah-h-h, that feels good," Jack said. "I always do that as soon as I get out of there." Studying the names and addresses on his packages, he started to move away. "Okay, so you two deliver those parcels and go home for tonight. Come back tomorrow night, about the same time. I'll be waiting for you. I'll get you into the warehouse again. I'll have your money for you too, for tonight's work."

"Sure thing," Vance called to Jack's retreating back as he watched him sprint to Main Street and disappear around the corner. "I didn't even get a chance to say thank you," he muttered, scratching his head and looking after him. "That's a fine how-do-you-do."

Andrea laughed in spite of herself. "What a funny thing to say!" She yawned largely, covering her mouth with one of the paper-wrapped packages. "I'm getting tired, Vance. Let's get these parcels delivered and then go back to Rosie's." She dragged her feet, suddenly realizing that she hadn't done what she'd set out to do. She still had no clue where Kami and Eddie might be.

"Don't worry too much about Kami," Vance said, nudging her with his shoulder, as if he could read her mind. "We couldn't have done anything tonight anyway."

"I guess not," Andrea sighed. She was cranky and already tired of playing this dangerous game. She just wanted to be home safe in her own house.

"Okay, let's get this job done." Vance took note of the addresses on Andrea's and his packages and then steered Andrea in the direction of their deliveries. Luckily, the packages only had to be delivered to the Hazelton Hotel, just across the street. They quickly delivered the parcels, receiving a nice tip from the desk clerk, and headed back to Rosie's place.

"I'm really beat," Vance admitted with a yawn as they neared the three-storey house Rosie called home. "I have to get up early to sell newspapers tomorrow."

"Thank you, Vance," Andrea whispered as she turned up the walk. "Thank you for believing me about the Chinese people, and for helping me. I wouldn't be able to do this without you." Vance clapped her once on the shoulder and then disappeared into the night.

Slipping silently through the doors, Andrea headed up the stairs toward Rosie's place. Exhaustion weighed heavily on her limbs and she found it difficult to lift her feet up each stair. Was she wearing lead shoes? She crept into the kitchen, trying hard to tiptoe. She didn't want to disturb the others.

Guiltily, she realized that she hadn't given them a thought since she'd left hours before. She hoped they'd gotten along well. It was hard staying with someone who obviously didn't trust or like you. Quietly opening the door to the spare bedroom, Andrea peeked inside.

Tony lay sprawled on the bed under a thin sheet, one leg flung out over the edge of the mattress. Baby Alan was asleep in his small bed, his little bottom sticking up in the air. Good, Tony was here. At least he'd listened to Andrea and not gone running off into the tunnels alone. Relieved, she pulled the door shut.

As Andrea turned, the other bedroom door opened. Sarah stood in the doorway in a long cotton nightgown, her hair caught up in a loose bun. The moon poured white light into the open window as a slight breeze ruffled the thin curtains. The two girls stared at one another for a few moments; it was almost as if they were sizing each other up.

"I know we haven't gotten off to a good start." Sarah finally said. She plaited her fingers together as she spoke. "I'm very puzzled by you and your brother. You're strangers here, but it's more than that, and I can't figure out what it is. And just when I was accepting you, you go and cut your hair!" She paused for a moment shaking her head.

"But I've decided that any friends of Rosie's are friends of mine, even if they are a bit odd." She smiled shyly, her eyes begging Andrea to understand. "And I wouldn't go to the police, even if I said I would."

Grateful for Sarah's honesty and trust, Andrea gave her a quick hug of thanks. "You're a very generous person, Sarah," she said, following her into the dimly lit room.

140

"Is there any news of your friends?"

"No," Andrea sighed, her heart heavy. "I don't know what we're going to do." The need for sleep overcame her. "Good night, Sarah, and thanks for understanding."

"I didn't say I understood you – I don't. I just know that Rosie would be upset if she thought I'd been unneighbourly. You do seem harmless enough, even though you're strange."

Andrea smiled in spite of herself. "Harmless," she muttered, bemused. There was something familiar about Sarah. Half asleep, she let that thought slip away.

Quickly, Andrea shucked her dirty clothes in a heap on the floor, pulled on the nightgown that Sarah had lent her, and crawled into the clean bed. Sleep was upon her the moment her head hit the pillow, but not so quickly that she didn't have time to consider two thoughts that drifted into her brain. Was it that horrible mixture of smells that was making her so tired? Were they noxious? And who was Sarah? Why did she seem so darned familiar?

BACK ON MAIN STREET

It was late morning by the time Andrea roused herself from sleep. She could hear Tony out in the kitchen area pacing and muttering to himself. He must feel like a caged animal, she thought guiltily, as she jumped out of bed. He hadn't been out of the apartment since they'd arrived. He needed a chance to get out and stretch his legs, otherwise he might decide to take matters into his own hands and disappear into the tunnels without her permission.

They'd walk down Main Street, she decided, as she climbed back into her overalls and dirty work shirt. It would be fun to see old-fashioned Moose Jaw in the daylight, and they might get some clues as to where Eddie might be.

"Good morning," Andrea called as she pulled the

door open and walked into the kitchen.

"I thought you were going to sleep all day," Tony complained. He sat at the table finishing a breakfast of cheese and bread.

"Sorry." Andrea finger-combed her hair and pulled the cap on. "I'll just grab an apple for breakfast and we'll take a walk down Main Street. Here's some money we can spend. We got a tip last night from the desk clerk at the Hazelton Hotel."

"Yay!" Tony grabbed an apple off the counter and shoved it into her hands. "Let's go!"

"Where are Sarah and Baby Alan?" Andrea asked, looking around the empty kitchen.

"Sarah's taken him out for a walk. They seem to do a lot of that," he added, grabbing his backpack.

"What else is there to do in the 1920s? There's no TV, no video games, no computer."

Tony sighed. "Quit making me homesick. I'm beginning to miss my things."

Pushing back that ever-present nagging worry about the twins, Andrea followed Tony out the door and down the stairs. She was glad she didn't have to worry about locking the door and making sure she had a key. It seemed that very few people locked doors around here in the daytime. It sure was different in the present!

There wasn't much Andrea could do during the daylight hours, and going out with Tony was a great way to relieve boredom. Besides, she loved walking around in the 1920s, pretending she belonged. She just hoped it wouldn't be permanent! And who knew? They might discover something important.

Pausing at the intersection of Main and River Street, Tony studied the downtown core of 1920s Moose Jaw. The train station loomed just one block ahead, the immense structure reaching into the bright blue sky.

Right in front of them, on the northwest corner of River Street, stood a brick building with large plate glass windows framed with wood. Most of the building was taken up by a quaint café. The most interesting thing about the building was the fact that the entrance wasn't built into either side of the building, but right on the corner where the two sides met. A sign over the door read "Wong's Café."

Sarah was pushing the pram across the street, waving at them to catch their attention. She had Vance and Beanie in tow. "We thought we'd take Baby Alan for an ice cream treat," she announced as they stopped in front of the door. She stooped to grab an excited Alan out of the pram. He was chortling loudly, pointing at the entrance to the café.

"You must bring him here often," Vance observed, his eyebrows lifting as he teased her.

Blushing, she shrugged her shoulders, averting her eyes. "Well, he does love ice cream, after all." Vance pushed open the door and let Sarah and Alan enter ahead of him.

"Oh brother," Beanie said, looking after them. "Looks like Vance is getting soft over Sarah."

"What?" Tony was puzzled.

"Vance likes Sarah," Andrea interpreted. She wasn't sure she liked the idea any better than Beanie did. After all, what did they really know about her?

"I'm going in. Are you coming?" Andrea pulled the cap low over her eyes and disappeared inside with Beanie following closely behind.

Studying River Street, Tony watched with interest as a Model T car chugged its way around the corner. Two delivery buggies pulled by horses moved by, the horses' hooves clicking rhythmically on the ground. Halfway down the block, a truck was backed up to the entrance of a building. It looked like a hotel. Men scurried about carrying wooden crates from the truck and into the entrance. They were Chinese men working in daylight. They must have paid their Head Tax. One of the workers looked familiar. Was it Eddie?

Tony hurried up the street as the worker disappeared inside. It sure looked like Eddie. He broke into a run. Screeching to a halt at the entrance, he dodged around the workers and stepped into the building. "Eddie?" he called. "Eddie? Is that you?"

"Get lost, kid. You don't know anybody here."

Mean-Eyed Max stood blocking the way, his muscular arms crossed over a massive chest.

"Where's Eddie?" Tony asked, craning his neck to peer behind the tree-stump legs. He stretched his body as long as it would go, hoping to appear taller. Although he was shaking with fear and his knees trembled, he tried to sound brave. He puffed up his chest and glared up at the mountain of a man, his arms akimbo, fists digging into his sides.

Mean-Eyed Max laughed a booming laugh that echoed around the lobby. "I could blow you over with one puff," he chortled. "I'm the Big Bad Wolf!"

He blew hot, stinky breath into Tony's face, trying to intimidate him, but Tony stood his ground. "Where's Eddie?" he repeated, trying to make his voice fierce.

"Which Eddie? Most of the coolies around here are named Eddie. They must like our English name. Why are you looking for a coolie, kid?"

"Eddie's my friend," Tony insisted, pointing down a long, dark hallway to where he thought Eddie had most likely disappeared. "I saw him come in here."

Mean-Eyed Max leaned toward him, strong fingers pressing against Tony's chest. His bulging eye stared straight at Tony, glassy and lifeless. "I said we don't have anyone named Eddie here." He spoke in a menacing voice that sent chills running down the backs of Tony's legs. "Now get lost, or I'll make mincemeat out of you!" Lunging, his arm coiled out and he grabbed Tony's backpack. "I've got you now."

Terrified, Tony lurched away, but he was like a dog caught by the leash; the backpack tethered him to the spot. Lashing out, he swung his fists wildly about, connecting with Mean-Eyed Max's soft belly.

"Oaff!" Mean-Eyed Max groaned, as his grip on the backpack weakened.

Feeling the slack, Tony jerked free and ran out the open door. He collided with one of the workers, who was entering the building carrying a wooden box. It crashed to the ground, the lid popping off. Yellow apples erupted, rolling around them.

"Excuse me," Tony apologized, tripping over the apples as he tried to escape.

"Stop him!" Mean-Eyed Max yelled from inside the building. Tony heard the sound of the door crashing against the wall and there stood Mean-Eyed Max breathing heavily, balled fists clenched at his waist. "I'm going to get you!"

Tony scrambled to get away from his long reach, his feet skating on the loose apples. Mean-Eyed Max lunged toward him, taking a huge step. His enormous foot landed on the edge of an apple. It skittered sideways and Max teetered, trying to catch his balance. He fell heavily, landing on his knees. "Oww!" he howled in pain, grabbing at his leg. "My knee."

"Get that kid," he roared, crawling toward the

147

doorway. He used the window frame to support his weight, as he poked his head into the doorway yelling for help.

Realizing this was his chance, Tony turned to scurry away, falling on the apples again. A hand reached up and pulled him to his feet. Tony found himself staring into the friendly face of a tall Chinese man.

The man wore a long black coat; a black derby perched on his head. He turned his head as he listened to the loud ranting voice inside the building. "Where's that kid?" Mean-Eyed Max bellowed.

The Chinese man bowed hurriedly, bending at the waist, hands pressed together at his chest, then grabbed Tony's hand. "Come with me. I will keep you safe."

THE MYSTERY MAN

"Am-am I being kidnapped?" Tony stammered as he bounced along. His hand was caught in the man's tight grip and he had no choice but to follow along.

The man almost ran down River Street, Tony flying along beside him. "Wh-where are you taking me?" he demanded, the words stammering out as he bounced along.

"We *must* hurry," the man said, looking over his shoulder. "Mr. Maxwell has not seen us, yet. This is so risky; I hope I am not making a mistake by helping you."

They reached the alley that ran behind the Main Street buildings and turned the corner into it. The man moved along the brick wall of the first building.

His hand reached out and pushed against the bricks. An invisible door slid open and he dragged Tony inside, swiftly closing the door behind them.

"Are you kidnapping me?" Tony asked again, as he stood in a dark, narrow passage. He was trembling almost uncontrollably.

The man laughed softly and then put his fingers to his lips. "Listen," he whispered, pressing his ear against the door they had just entered.

Holding his breath, Tony tried to quiet his pounding heart. Muffled sounds came from the alley and he recognized the voice of Mean-Eyed Max. They were looking for him!

"Don't worry," the Chinese man reassured Tony. "They won't find you here. I am very secretive; they don't know about my tunnels and hidden passageways." The sounds from the alley faded and the man escorted Tony further into the building. "I overheard your confrontation with Mr. Maxwell. You are looking for a friend?"

Tony nodded. "I'm looking for my friend, Eddie. Eddie Mark."

"Eddie Mark." Turning, the man studied Tony for a moment in the dim light. "You call a Chinese person a friend. You are brave. I saw you stand up to Mr. Maxwell. I need someone to help me. I need someone with courage. I need you, little one. People are often suspicious of me because I'm Chinese. You would fit right in and go unnoticed into places where I would draw unwanted attention to myself."

"What kind of help do you need?" Tony asked excitedly. "Does it have anything to do with saving Eddie from that awful place? Where are we anyway? And who are you?" He scanned the cramped passageway. It was very much like a tunnel, only it was above ground.

The man smiled. "Patience, boy. Patience. My name is Mr. Wong. I own this café."

"What café?" Tony asked, looking around him. "All I see is a spooky tunnel."

The man laughed again, the merry sound bouncing in Tony's ears. "This is the back of the café. My home is here. The café is in front. It faces Main Street."

"You own a café," Tony said, his eyes huge. "You must be rich!"

Mr. Wong laughed. "No, I'm not rich. I worked hard and saved my money. I came to Canada as an indentured servant. I worked for five years to pay the company for my passage and then I worked another four years to pay the Head Tax. Last year I finally had enough money to pay for my wife and two children to come to Canada, and we are a family again. Now I am in the position of being able to help other people like me."

"My family is getting ice cream in your café right now! Wouldn't they be surprised to know where I am!"

"But you must never tell them about this," Mr. Wong said, his voice serious. "There are many people to protect."

"I understand," Tony said, nodding.

"And what's your name?"

"Tony."

Mr. Wong studied Tony again. "You look trustworthy and honest. Can you keep a secret?"

"I can," Tony nodded eagerly, pressing his lips tightly together to show his sincerity.

Standing quietly for several moments, Mr. Wong again studied Tony. "In that case, young Tony, let me show you some of my secrets."

Mr. Wong led the way through the passage until they came to a door. It opened silently and they stepped into the most beautiful room Tony had ever seen. It was draped with colourful pieces of flowing material that Tony guessed was silk. Chinese artwork dotted the walls, and lamps sat on low tables, the shades made out of fragile material that looked like paper. Tony felt as if he was actually in China! He could hear the happy chatter of two young Chinese voices in the next room, and the patient, calmer replies of a woman. That must be Mr. Wong's family, he guessed.

Only a large wooden table, set in one corner of the room, was out of place. It looked too Canadian, but it was functional. A teenaged Chinese boy sat at the table writing something. "Is that your son?"

Mr. Wong shook his head. "No, but come and meet him. He will be happy to speak to a real Canadian."

"Kim," Mr. Wong said, clearly pronouncing the words. "This is our new friend, Tony."

Grinning, Kim bowed. "Pleased," he said, bending over his hands. "Pleased to meet you."

His accent was so strong that Tony could barely understand him. "What are you working on?" he asked, glancing down at Kim's work.

Proudly, Kim shoved the paper toward Tony. "You, read," he said, pointing to his work.

Picking the paper up, Tony studied the carefully made letters. "A," he read. "The apple is red. B. The baby cries. C. The cat meows."

"You're teaching him English!"

"Yes," Mr. Wong smiled. "Reading and writing. How else can one get along in a new country?"

"If he's not your son, is he your nephew?"

"Nephew?" Mr. Wong questioned. He still had trouble with some English words, even though he spoke English very well now.

"You know," Tony said, trying to think of how to explain the word. Is he your – your sister or brother's son?"

Gesturing, Mr. Wong encouraged Kim to speak. "You tell Tony how we are connected."

"I am not related," Kim said, struggling to find the

right words. "Mr. Wong is my friend. He saved me from that big bad man. He is teaching me English. He is helping me to pay my Head Tax."

"Oh," Tony said, his eyes huge as he took in all the information. "You mean, you're rescuing the workers and helping them get a head start in Canada. Wow! That's neat!"

"I can only take a few at a time. I have to be careful and I have to make sure I can support the number of people I take. I have my wife and children to consider as well. I can't put them into danger. I am always wishing that I could do more." He sighed.

"Oh well," Tony tried to comfort him. "At least you're helping some people. That's a start."

"Yes, it is," Mr. Wong agreed. "I like you, young Tony. You have a good heart. Your family must be proud of you."

Smiling, Tony wondered what Mr. Wong would think if he told him just what was happening with his family right now; how he was back in time visiting with his teenaged grandpa and great aunt Bea. "You know, I've probably been gone for a long time. They're going to be looking for me. I'd better be getting back. But first, Mr. Wong, you can help Eddie, right?"

"Yes," Mr. Wong assured. "I can help Eddie, but I'm going to need your help to do it. I need your assurance too, that you won't tell anyone about what you've seen here."

"Not anyone?" Tony questioned. A picture of Andrea flashed through his mind and he felt bad. He wasn't used to keeping secrets from her. It didn't feel right, somehow.

"The more people who know about this, the more danger we are in," Mr. Wong said. "You must keep it a secret."

Reluctantly, Tony agreed. How was he going to keep a secret from Andrea? She could read him like a book.

Mr. Wong showed Tony the way out. "I'll see you again soon. If you need me, you can always ask for me in the café."

"Okay," Tony agreed. He said goodbye and then Mr. Wong opened the door a crack and Tony slid out into the alley again. He expected it to be night, for it felt as if he had been gone for a long time. But the bright afternoon sun shone down upon him as he turned the corner of the building onto River Street.

"Where's Tony?" he heard Andrea's voice float toward him. She held Baby Alan in her arms as she frantically searched Main Street, trying to catch a glimpse of him.

"Here I am," Tony called as he joined the group from behind. Everyone had been so busy watching Main Street, that no one saw him come up from behind.

"Where have you been?" Andrea demanded, whirling around to face him.

"I've been here, all the time," Tony answered, somewhat truthfully. "I was just walking on River Street, and I saw Eddie," Tony burst out, hoping to distract Andrea. Baby Alan was perched in her arms, looking around with bright eyes. "I know I saw Eddie. He went inside that building!" He pointed down River Street.

Andrea looked at the nondescript brick building. "Tony, you can't just run off and leave us like that! And we promised to stay off River Street, remember?"

Looking around the street, Andrea noticed several scruffy and scary-looking men lounging against buildings and doorposts nearby, watching their every move. Women in interesting clothes leaned out of windows in the brick buildings, waving and calling to the men. Everything about River Street gave her the creeps. "Come on, let's get back to Main Street."

"But what about Eddie?" Tony insisted, looking as if he wanted to run back and kick the door open.

"He'll be long gone by now. Are you sure it was him, Tony?"

"Yes, I'm sure."

"Take a good look at that building," Andrea said, glancing back at it for a moment. "Wing's Grocery" its sign said. She shifted Baby Alan to her other arm; he was getting heavy. "We may need to come back here again. If only we knew for sure whether it was Eddie or not." She sighed. "I wonder why it looks so – so – "

"Seedy," Beanie supplied, coming up behind them with two ice cream cones. Some of it was beginning to run down her fingers. Licking the surplus from the side of the cone, she handed it to Baby Alan. "That's what my mother calls it. It's probably because they're doing illegal things."

"Yeah," Tony agreed. "Why else would Mean-Eyed Max be guarding that place?"

"You just saw Mean-Eyed Max?" Andrea shivered, glad that she had been the one bringing up the rear with Baby Alan and the others.

"It's really scary down here. Let's get back to Main Street." Beanie led the way. "Rosie won't be too happy if she finds out that we brought Baby Alan to River Street." But the baby wasn't paying any attention to his surroundings. All of his interest was focused on the ice cream treat he had clutched in his tiny hands. Strawberry ice cream was smeared across his face and dripping off his chin and on to Andrea's flannel shirt. He was making a mess!

"Sarah won't be happy with us, either," Andrea added, trying to wipe ice cream from her shirt. Both Vance and Sarah stood at the corner, their arms crossed, frowning at them. "I think we're in trouble."

Sarah lectured them all the way home about taking Baby Alan only to respectable places. They apologized again and again, promising to be more careful.

Reaching Rosie's house, Sarah carried the baby up the walk for his afternoon nap.

"You didn't get any ice cream," Beanie said to Tony, suddenly looking remorseful. "Why don't we go back and get you one?"

"Nah," Tony said. "I wasn't planning on getting any. I shouldn't have it unless I plan for it." He smiled inside, proud that he could now say that and not feel slighted.

"You can't eat ice cream?" Beanie looked surprised and then she remembered. "Oh, the sugar. I forgot. I'm sorry. I shouldn't have eaten mine in front of you."

"It's okay," Tony said. He searched inside himself and was happy to find out that it was the truth. It was all right, at least today. Another day he might feel bad that he couldn't eat what everyone else was having, but today it didn't matter. Today he had more important things on his mind. Like Eddie and Kim and his new friend, Mr. Wong.

There were all kinds of heroes in the world, he decided, but most people just knew about the popular and well-known heroes. He realized that there were quiet heroes who just did something because it needed doing; someone who helped people just because they needed the help.

Mr. Wong was one of those kinds of heroes, and Tony was glad he had met him. He hoped he would be able to help Mr. Wong rescue Eddie and maybe a few more of the workers who were trapped in those terrible conditions. He wondered, though, just how they would accomplish it with so many bad guys around.

THE CATASTROPHE

The next night Andrea and Vance entered the laundry with the other delivery boys. Walking slowly among the workers in the laundry area, she searched for Kami. At the end of the area she neared the huge stoves and paused to peer into a large soup pot. Simmering inside was a greyish soup with anemic pieces of what looked to be vegetables floating on the surface. She gagged on the smell and quickly turned away, glad she didn't have to eat that – whatever it was.

Suddenly from the laundry area came the sound of a booming crash. Nearly jumping out of her skin in fright, Andrea grabbed the corner of the nearest table to keep from falling. Blood-curdling screams rent the air. She flew across the floor to see what had happened.

Loud voices shouted in confusion as Stanford pushed his way into the centre of the crowd. Pressing close, Andrea peered over shoulders and around bodies and caught a glimpse of one of the workers lying on the floor in a pool of steaming water. "Don't look," Vance warned her, coming up from behind. Wrenching her arm, he pulled her out of the crowd and away from the accident.

"What happened?" she demanded, twisting back and pulling away to get another look.

"One of those huge laundry tubs tipped, scalding a worker. Andrea, he's hurt very badly. Don't look," Vance pleaded, pulling her by the arms toward the exit.

"It might be Kami!" That awful thought galvanized her into action. She had to know. Giving a mighty jerk, she managed to pull away from Vance. Whirling around, she ran back, quickly pushing her way through the crowd of wailing Chinese workers and silent delivery boys. Scalding hot water was everywhere, pooling around their feet, centimetres deep. The soles of her shoes warmed at once and a burning sensation irritated the bottoms of her feet.

A young Chinese worker lay unconscious on the floor. It was a girl. Her clothes were soaked, steam rising from them in wispy puffs that hung in the air around her. Two of the workers began to pull frantically at her clothes, trying to get her out of the hot

161

garments. Two others had run for a flat board, which they lifted her onto and carried her away. Would they get her a doctor? Who would care for this poor person?

Whether or not it was a combination of the noxious fumes and the sight of the wounded worker, Andrea didn't know, but suddenly she felt as if she might be sick. She dragged herself away from the horrible scene looking for a place to throw up in private.

Moving away from the crowd of people standing around the overturned laundry tub, Andrea headed back toward the door and the office platform. The area was empty and she managed to reach the steps leading toward the office door. Slumping forward, clutching her stomach, she leaned against the wooden railing, taking deep breaths. Fine perspiration broke out on her forehead. She needed help now, before she fainted.

Suddenly, a small hand appeared, guiding a tiny cup to her lips. Soft words calmed her nerves as she sipped the liquid. A sharp taste, which she recognized, filled her mouth. Her mother had always said that green tea calmed an upset stomach. "Kami?" she asked, looking for the person who had handed her the tea.

"Andrea? Is that you?! You look like a boy! Am I ever glad to see you!" Kami reached out to embrace her, her face shining with happiness and relief. "I thought I'd be stuck down here forever!"

"What's going on here?" a loud voice roared in Andrea's ear and she almost jumped out of her skin for the second time. Kami disappeared back into the crowd of workers, vanishing so fast Andrea wasn't sure she'd actually seen her. Her stomach did flip-flops and she felt herself grow faint again. Turning, she found Stanford towering over her, his eyes glinting dangerously.

"He's just upset by the accident, sir," Vance panted, coming up behind her and dropping parcels into Andrea's shaking hands. "He'll be all right, though, won't you Andr-Andy." The crisp paper packages crackled as she squeezed tightly, holding them against her squirming stomach. Nodding, she felt as if all the blood in her body had suddenly dropped to her feet, pooling there and leaving her light-headed.

Stanford stared at Andrea a moment longer through eyes like narrow slits of anger and suspicion. "Well, get moving or we'll hire other workers. These kinds of accidents happen all the time. What's the loss of a coolie or two!"

Andrea was horrified by his inhumanity and wished that she could tell him so, but to open her mouth would have brought disaster. She let the moment pass, silently biting her lips and keeping her thoughts captive.

Stanford must have read her mind. Glaring at her, he waved a beefy fist in her direction. "Leave the coolies alone! They don't speak English and we want to keep it that way! Stay away from the coolies! Understand?"

Nodding mutely, Andrea pulled herself to her feet. Weaving her way through the basement, she quickly climbed the terrible steps and half fell out into the warehouse area. Her heart sang, even as she beat her queasy stomach into submission. She had seen Kami! Finally, at last, they had proof that Kami was there, but someone had been hurt very badly. It was all just too much to take in all at once and her emotions flip-flopped like frogs at a jumping contest.

"That was a close call," Vance said as he caught up to her. "We'd better be more careful from now on, about everything. The water could spill on us too, you know."

Wanting to sing and dance, yet feeling immensely sad and still in shock, Andrea struggled to remain calm. "I saw her, Vance!"

"What?" He jerked to a stop, whipping his head around to stare at her in the dusky warehouse. "Are you sure?"

"Yes," Andrea nodded. "I really, really saw her. She was the one who gave me tea when I felt so sick. It all happened so fast, it's almost as if I imagined it all." Vance was so quiet that Andrea nudged him. "Did you hear me?"

"Yes, but Andrea, I didn't see anybody near you.

Honest. Are you sure you didn't just dream it all up because you want it to happen so badly?"

Confused, she closed her eyes for a minute, trying to recall everything that had taken place. Or had it? It was a jumble in her mind: the accident; the horror of seeing the wounded person lying so motionless that she looked dead; then seeing Kami. Or had she?

What if she was wrong and Vance was right? What if she just wanted it to be Kami so desperately that she dreamed up the whole incident? Swallowing hard, Andrea tried to think. Then she smiled. "It was Kami," she said with confidence as she headed toward the warehouse door. "I know it was." She could still taste the strong green tea on her tongue. That was her proof. She had seen Kami. Now they just had to figure out a way to rescue her.

Andrea was so engrossed in her thoughts that she didn't hear Vance's whispered warning that trouble was ahead. Looming out of the darkness, shadows making his gigantic features more grotesque than ever, stomped Mean-Eyed Max. He roared, arms waving in the air as he stormed across the floor so quickly that there was no chance to escape. He stopped right in front of them and stood glowering at them, his lips curled in a sneer, his glass eye bulging and twitching in anger.

Andrea's stomach clenched in terror. Whether it was because of Mean-Eyed Max, the after-affects of the nausea she had been feeling, or the horror of the accident, she could never say. Much to her dread and horror, her stomach revolted. It gave one mighty heave and she lost its entire contents in one swift motion – all over Mean-Eyed Max's shiny shoes.

MORE EXCITEMENT
AT THE LAUNDRY

Laughing weakly and crying at the same time, Andrea leaned against the wall of the warehouse. "I can't believe I did that," she hiccupped, rubbing her sore stomach.

"Me either," Vance said grimly, shaking his head. He looked like he was about to lecture her. His index finger was pointed in her direction, his blue eyes serious. Then his eyes began to twinkle and a smile played at his lips. Laughter erupted from deep within and his shoulders shook. "What a story we'll have to tell, someday!"

"But who would believe us?" Andrea asked, sighing. "I'm just glad I got to know you as a young person too, Grandpa. I'm lucky, even if I am in danger."

Vance pulled her close for a brief hug. "And I'm lucky too," he said gruffly, sounding just like Grandpa Talbot. He cleared his throat. "How are you feeling?"

"I'm okay," Andrea said, and she was. Her energy was returning and her stomach had finally settled down.

"I think we should go back inside now to rescue Kami."

"Now?" Andrea squeaked in surprise. "Why now?"

"Because there's a lot of confusion going on. I think we'd be able to sneak Kami out without anyone noticing." He grabbed her hand, chuckling. "Besides, did you see how upset Mean-Eyed Max was about his shoes? He didn't even think about us! He just yelled for water and took off toward the office. He's probably busy washing his shoes off!"

"It's a good thing he didn't think about us," Andrea added, breathing deeply to calm her nerves. "He would have caught me for sure! I was frozen to the spot. I'm glad you dragged me out of there! Maybe you're right, though, maybe we should go back in now."

"I am right," Vance declared. "Let's go."

They stashed their packages of clean laundry against the side of the warehouse and Andrea followed Vance back down the moonlit street toward the warehouse door. Going back now, when everything was still in chaos, was a good idea. Maybe they could just spirit Kami away and no one would be the wiser. That seemed like the best plan and Andrea hoped it would work. With the two of them, it should be easier, since one could distract unwanted attention, or scout ahead to see if it was safe to leave.

Looking off in the distance, Vance spotted a few of the boys returning. "There are some of the fellas coming back right now. If we hurry, we can go into the warehouse with them." Breaking into a run, he jogged toward the huge building.

Andrea had to run hard to catch up, her breath coming in sharp gasps. Vance was a good runner! She'd have to remember to tell her grandfather, when she got back to the present again. Tiny prickles of homesickness suddenly attacked, and she wished that she was home again with everyone safe around her. This rescue operation was so dangerous, but she had no choice. She had to save Kami and Eddie. Resolutely pushing back her homesick thoughts, she hurried to catch up to Vance.

Everyone converged on the warehouse door at once and pushed through into the darkness as a large group. They ambled past Mean-Eyed Max's office and Andrea breathed easier when she saw it was empty. Maybe he had gone out for a while. Maybe he had gone to clean his shoes! Despite the graveness of their situation, she had to smile at that thought.

They passed the spot where her unfortunate incident had taken place. The air was still pungent with the strong odour. Several boys commented quietly, covering their noses as they hurried by. Andrea felt her face grow red and was thankful for the cover of darkness to hide her embarrassment.

The trip back to the laundry area was easy and uneventful, but chaos still reigned there. The victim was nowhere to be seen. The laundry tub had been righted and was being refilled with water. The floor was still wet and workers pushed the excess water toward the drain, away from the busy washing area. Stanford stood, leaning on the wooden mop handle, watching everyone else work.

Scanning the workers, Andrea searched for Kami, but with so many people milling about it was impossible to spot her. She caught Vance's eye and shook her head. He shrugged his shoulders, a blank look on his face. How could Vance help to recognize her, Andrea wondered, when he'd never met her before.

They fanned out, taking a casual walk into the eating area. Andrea went first, looking carefully at all of the workers seated at the wooden tables. Some were eating the horrible-looking gruel, while others wrote what appeared to be letters — long pieces of paper with beautiful Chinese characters etched across. She wondered what kind of information they passed on to their loved ones in China. Surely they didn't talk about the horrid living and working conditions.

Maybe they wrote about hopes and dreams, the hope of making enough money to pay their Head Tax and get real jobs, and the dream of being together again. The sadness and shame of their plight brought tears to Andrea's eyes and she quickly blinked them away, pushing back those melancholy thoughts. She couldn't concentrate on that right now; she had to find Kami.

Suddenly, Kami appeared right before her eyes. "Kami!" Andrea exclaimed, grabbing the girl's arm.

"Thank goodness you came back!" Kami whispered, squeezing Andrea's hand in a death grip. "I was almost ready to escape myself, but I thought I should wait for you! I wanted to see Ming once more, not to say goodbye," she hurriedly added, "just to say thanks for being my friend. But I can't find her. I wonder where she is?" Worry filled her eyes. "I hope she wasn't the one who got hurt."

Vance came up quickly from behind. "You're not saying a word to anyone. The fewer people who know about this, the better." He shuffled the girls back through the kitchen area toward the underground storage area and the tunnels.

"Most people are busy cleaning. Stanford is still over there inspecting the mess," Vance whispered. The workers at the tables were too weary to lift their eyes and witness their escape. "Just keep moving toward the stairs. I think we'll make it! I'm Vance, by the way," he said. Kami nodded.

"Okay, now comes the hard part," Vance murmured, his words laced with anxiety. "I'll scout around and see if the coast is clear." Leaving Andrea and Kami huddled in a dark corner near the stairs, he hurried away. Kami fell silent, watching him go.

Back within seconds, although it seemed like an eternity to Andrea, Vance took Kami by the elbow, escorting her toward the door leading to the underground storage area. "I can't believe our luck," he said, grinning over his shoulder at Andrea. "This is too easy!"

Vance spoke too soon.

They were within two metres of the door when it was suddenly flung open. There, grunting up the three steps, his back to them, was Mean-Eyed Max. He was struggling to drag something huge and heavy in through the door. Andrea let out a high squeak of terror as her limbs became petrified with fear. She stood frozen to the spot.

"Give me a hand here, eh?" Mean-Eyed Max glanced briefly over his shoulder. Thinking fast, Andrea grabbed Kami and pulled her behind a stack of wooden boxes.

"I ain't got all day!" Mean-Eyed Max roared. "This thing is heavy!"

"S-sure," Vance agreed, moving as slowly as possible toward Mean-Eyed Max.

"Where's your friend?" Mean-Eyed Max shouted, pitching his head back. "I thought I saw two of you." His beady eyes pinpointed Andrea in a second. "Hey! You're the one who puked all over my shoes! I owe you one! Get over here and help – NOW!!"

His horrid tone of voice pushed Andrea into action. Grabbing Kami's hand she fled toward the rickety steps, leaving Vance to face the wrath of Mean-Eyed Max alone. Luckily his swearing and calling for help couldn't be heard by anyone; the clamouring noise from the laundry area was too loud. Andrea still had a chance to save Kami, if only Vance could keep Mean-Eyed Max occupied long enough.

Andrea looked behind and Vance caught her eye and smiled. She watched as he knocked against a huge pile of wooden boxes as he went by. They fell to the floor with a clatter, right in Max's way. That should keep them busy for a while!

Thankfully, no one was coming down the stairs. "You go first," Andrea directed. She would bring up the rear, pushing Kami, if she needed to. Slow and clumsy on the stairs, perhaps because she was afraid, Kami seemed to take forever. Impatiently, Andrea pushed and prodded, begging and pleading with her to hurry. She could still hear Mean-Eyed Max cussing and carrying on about the mess of boxes in his way and ordering Vance to help clean them up.

At the top of the stairs, Andrea pushed past Kami,

grabbing her wrist. Listening at the outside door, she carefully pushed it open. The sound of voices reached her. Recognizing them instantly, she felt sick. Chubbs and Stilts! Why did they always show up at the worst possible time?

Andrea pulled Kami into the shadows as the two men entered the warehouse area.

"I'm going downstairs," Stilts called. "You stay here!"

Andrea could hear the sound of Stilts as he clumped down the stairs, but she couldn't see where Chubbs had got to. Oh, what was she to do? Should they risk running back to the front door?

Without taking time to think of a plan of action, Andrea pulled Kami further away from the doorway, further into the darkness of the warehouse. At least they were now at ground level. They just needed to find a door that led to the outside. "Look for a way out of here," Andrea said softly, her heading swiveling in every direction, searching for the elusive Chubbs.

"I am," Kami whispered, her hands clutching Andrea's overalls. "I'm looking so hard I feel like my eyes are going to pop out of my head!"

Something crunched under Andrea's feet. "Hey, what's this?" Bending down, she picked up a crumpled piece of paper.

"It looks like it's got numbers and dates on it," Kami whispered, peering at the paper. "It's too dark to read exactly what it says."

Andrea shoved it into her pocket. "I think it's a page from some kind of log book. We'll look at it later. It might give us a clue to what's going on around here. Let's just find a way out for now!" Grabbing Kami's hand once more, she moved toward the far wall, suddenly remembering that there had been a door leading into the back alley behind the building.

Deep shadows merged around piles of boxes and furniture, and Andrea knew it would be easy to become lost and disoriented. Was there really another door? She searched frantically for a place for them to hide.

"Look, Andrea!" Kami pointed excitedly.

In the back corner, Andrea thought she could see light filtering in. Stumbling over a small box, she noisily kicked it aside and flew toward the light source, dragging Kami with her. It was a door! "Come on, Kami," she said, trying to push it open.

"It's stuck," Kami was energized with fear, her feet kicking against the stubborn door. This was almost more than Andrea could handle. Tears of worry, pain, and frustration began to gather in her eyes and she blinked rapidly. Don't cry now, she begged, kicking at the door. You can do this! But it was obvious that the door was stuck – or locked.

Clattering sounds came from the direction of the stairs and Andrea knew that her time was up.

Someone was coming after them! It was now or never. Fleetingly, she wondered what they would do to her when they discovered that she was trying to steal one of their workers. Whatever it was, she knew it wouldn't be pleasant.

"Looks like you're in quite a predicament."

Andrea whirled around at the softly spoken words, her heart in her throat. Even Kami sensed danger, for she quit beating on the door and instead, shrank back against it, speechless with terror.

"Help us, please." Andrea stared at her captor – or was he her deliverance from this terrible mess? She couldn't see him clearly, although his voice sounded familiar. She had nothing to lose by begging for his help; she was down to her last bit of luck. "If they catch us, I'm in a lot of trouble!"

Tilting his head, he listened as the men reached the top of the stairs. In the whisper of light trickling in, Andrea recognized Jack. What would he do?

He too, seemed to be asking that question, for he stared for at Andrea and then Kami for a long moment. "Do you know what you're doing?" he finally asked. "She's a coolie."

Kami was mute, staring at Jack. She knew her future rested squarely in his hands.

Andrea nodded. "She's a coolie," she agreed, "but it's not what you think."

Making his decision, Jack reached behind and

above her, fumbling with something in the darkness. Andrea heard a small click and the door slid open, revealing the backs of buildings. Fresh air rushed in as Andrea pushed Kami out into the alley. "You can't save them all," Jack told her, shaking his head. "There are too many and no one cares what happens to them. What are you going to do with this one?"

"Ask Vance some day," Andrea panted, as she pulled Kami further into the alley. "And thank you, Jack. Perhaps someday I can tell you what you've just done." He nodded once and then closed the door firmly, locking them outside in the quiet Moose Jaw night.

"We're not safe, yet," Andrea told Kami, pulling her away from the building. She tripped over a long white bundle lying next to the building and nearly fell. Glancing back curiously to see what it was, she froze in mid-step, and then not quite believing, she blocked that gruesome thought with a long stream of words.

"Let's run up this alley behind Main Street and then circle back to Rosie's place. I'm sure they'll come looking for us soon, and I don't want them to see us. We have to keep Sarah and everyone else out of this. I sure hope Vance is all right."

"Who are these people anyway?" Kami puffed. Andrea ignored her, hoping that there would be time for questions later, if they made it safely to Rosie's place.

They hastened up the alley and turned onto the street. As they disappeared around the corner, Andrea peered back at the building. No one had emerged from the warehouse, and she felt a load lift from her shoulders. Kami was rescued. Now there was just Eddie to worry about, as long as Vance stayed safe.

THE HOMECOMING

They got to Rosie's within minutes, and Andrea breathed a sigh of relief. "Where are we?" Kami asked, her face lit with joy. "I'm so happy to be free!" She threw her arms around Andrea, hugging her fiercely. "I was so scared down there! I thought I might be stuck there forever!

"Where's Eddie?" she asked, looking up at the Rosie's dark house. It was almost midnight and the windows facing the street were all black. "Is he safe?"

Andrea gently guided Kami inside and led her up the stairs. "We haven't found him yet, but we're working on it. This is Rosie's place, but I'll explain everything later. I sure wish Rosie was here."

As if by magic, the door at the top of the steps flew open and Rosie emerged, arms outstretched, a huge smile lighting her face. "Andrea!"

Andrea let herself be engulfed in Rosie's love as she nestled her head into the motherly shoulder and blinked rapidly to keep the tears at bay. "I'm so glad to see you, Rosie."

"And I'm glad to see you too. It looks like I got home just in the nick of time. I go away for a while and my time travelling friends come back again and get into a heap of trouble!

"Who have we here?" she asked, glimpsing Kami standing just behind Andrea, watching the joyful reunion.

"This is my friend, Kami," Andrea said, pulling away and reaching for Kami's hand. "Vance and I just rescued her."

"It's nice to meet you," Rosie said, reaching to pull Kami further into the room. "You must be hungry."

"I'm starving," Kami admitted hesitantly, staring around the room in wonder. She really was in the past! This room seemed so-so old-fashioned! And the woman too! "The food down there was awful. I could barely eat any of it."

"Sarah, put the baby down and get this girl something to eat," Rosie instructed. Sarah, looking utterly bewildered at the condition of Kami's clothes and the fact that she was Chinese, quickly complied.

Hearing all of the commotion, Tony came rushing out of the bedroom, his hair sleep-tousled. A huge smile split his face. "Kami!" He launched himself at her, almost knocking her over with an exuberant bear hug. "Am I glad to see you!"

Vance came tearing up the steps, sliding into the kitchen and dropping into a chair. "Whew! You're a sight for sore eyes!" Grinning at Andrea, he reached over to pat her shoulder. "I didn't know if you'd make it or not! I'm glad to see you're both safe and sound." He glanced at Kami briefly. "One rescued, and Rosie's here too!" He grabbed her up in a huge bear hug. "Welcome home! How do you do, Kami?"

Kami nodded, looking curiously at all the people. "You look awfully familiar," she said to Vance, gawking at him.

Vance and Andrea exchanged glances and burst out laughing.

"Sh-h-h," Sarah admonished them. "It's after midnight! People are trying to sleep!"

Rosie nodded in agreement, cuddling Alan. "I know you should be in bed, but I'm just so glad to see you!" She squeezed him tightly as he grabbed her hair and giggled with delight.

"You do know him," Tony snickered, "but you'll never guess who he is, not in a million years."

Shaking her head, Kami continued to study Vance, and Beanie too. "I give up," she finally conceded as Sarah placed a heaping bowl of stew in front of her.

"Kami, meet Vance, my grandfather!" Andrea announced like a barker at the circus. "And this is Great Aunt Bea!"

"Really?" Kami sighed. "It's just too much to believe. I mean, look at this room. I feel like I'm living in Boomtown in the Western Development Museum! Did we actually travel back in time?"

"Yes, we did. Isn't that incredible?"

"Yes," Kami said, dipping her spoon into the stew and then looking up, alarmed. "But what about my brother? Where's Eddie?"

"Don't worry," Vance assured her, patting her shoulder as she sat at the table. "We found you. We'll find Eddie too!"

"What were you talking about when you mentioned time travelling?" Sarah asked quietly.

Everyone in the kitchen froze, then cast furtive glances at one another. "I'll tell you about it later," Andrea hedged, now knowing that Sarah was trustworthy. "But first I need to talk to Rosie."

A happy and relaxed Rosie sat at the table, Baby Alan squirming on her lap. "Oh, I missed you." She planted kisses on his cheeks and all over the top of his head while he threaded his fingers through her frilly blouse and twisted it. "Okay, Andrea, tell me your story."

Andrea recounted the tale of Kami's rescue. As she got to the end, the long white bundle in the alley flashed into her mind. Now that she had time to think about it, she trembled.

Silently, they watched for a moment as Kami wolfed down her food. "That was delicious," she said, sitting back with a sigh of contentment. "Thank you." Looking down at her filthy outfit, she brushed ineffectually at some of the bigger stains. "Do you think I could have a bath?" she asked hesitantly. "I feel gross."

"Of course," Rosie said. "Sarah, get a towel for Kami and find her something of mine to wear. We'll have to wash her tunic," she said, eyeing the dark stains on Kami's clothes. "Show her where the bathroom is, Beanie. It's not as convenient as your modern ways – we share the bathroom with the other tenants. However, it will get you clean."

Sarah disappeared into Rosie's room and came back out a few moments later with a white towel and a bright red dress with large black polka dots. "This is all I could find."

Kami stared at the dress. It looked huge.

"She'll look like a circus clown in that!" Tony laughed, then he stifled a yawn. "I'm going back to bed. It's way too late for me to be up. Good night." He disappeared into the bedroom, closing the door behind him.

"Uh-h, thanks," Kami said again, not sure she was thankful for the dress, especially after Tony's teasing comment. At least she wouldn't have to wear it for long. Meekly she followed Beanie out of the apartment and down the stairs in search of the bathroom.

Andrea thought of the bundle in the alley again. "Are you looking for a newspaper article, Rosie?"

"I'm always on the hunt for a good story," Rosie replied, taking a plate of bread, fruit, and cheese from Sarah and setting it down on the table. "That's why I was in Regina."

"Now, Andrea, what's on your mind?" Rosie asked gently as the footsteps faded on the stairs.

"Yeah," Vance added, squeezing her shoulder as he slipped into the chair beside her. "You're trembling."

Andrea wrapped her arms around her chest, wondering if she would ever forget the feeling of tripping over the soft form on the ground behind the warehouse. "Have you got a photographer who can go with you, Rosie? You'll want to take a picture, quickly, before they move it."

"Move what?" Rosie stood, hands on her hips, curious and impatient at the same time.

"Well, if you really want your story, get that photographer quickly and go look behind the warehouse in the alley. Go before they move it," Andrea choked, fighting back tears.

"Move what?" Rosie asked again, placing a comforting hand on Andrea's shoulder.

"What's got you so upset?" Vance asked, his eyebrows knit with worry.

"I tripped over something in the alley just now as Kami and I were escaping," she sobbed, finally breaking into tears. "I think it's a dead body."

TONY GETS A JOB

Tony opened the bedroom door and tiptoed silently out into the kitchen carrying his shoes, his backpack securely on his back. He had waited in bed, the sheet pulled up to his chin, fully dressed, while the others talked and talked and talked in the kitchen. It seemed to him that it had been ages until Rosie had come quietly into the room, placing a sleeping Alan gently in bed and kissing him good night. Tony had feigned sleep, trying to make his breathing soft and even, his eyes fluttering open as Rosie pulled the door shut. Vance had left with Rosie, and the others had gone to bed. Tony had waited a full thirty minutes after he had heard Rosie and Vance call good night. He glanced at his digital watch. It was one thirty in the morning; surely everyone was asleep by now.

Now was his chance! Tony had promised to meet Mr. Wong at a secret rendezvous and he needed to get there soon. Holding his breath, he tiptoed across the quiet kitchen and opened the door. Stepping out onto the first stair, he pulled the door closed behind him and moved as silently as a shadow down the stairs and out into the street, hoping he wouldn't meet Rosie coming back in.

Luck was with him. The street was deserted. Tony sprinted to Main Street, the bright moon casting dark shadows around him as he ran. He needed to get into the tunnels again and he knew just where he could do that. Running to the brick hotel, he ran his hands along the wall. His fingers found a small clasp and he pulled it. The door opened onto the shaky spiral staircase.

Carefully he wound his way down the staircase, his only source of light a tiny pen flashlight, attached to his backpack. At the bottom, the tunnel began, a lantern sputtering nearby. He knew this was a short tunnel, which led to the Windy tunnel.

He moved cautiously, trying not to kick up the rocks and pebbles that crunched under his feet. Even with the lanterns lit, the tunnel was gloomy and Tony felt uncomfortable, as if the tunnel walls were closing in on him. This was the tunnel he had passed out in last year and it gave him the creeps.

Very soon he came to the intersection and turned into the tunnel that ran under Main Street. The sound of feet shuffling along in the gravel echoed through the tunnel, followed by the clanking noises of metal against metal. It sounded like a lot of people moving toward him. Finding a small hollowed-out spot at the edge of the tunnel, he squeezed his body into the small space, hoping he was invisible.

Stilts and Chubbs came into view with six Chinese workers. Chubbs led the group, while Stilts brought up the rear, a big stick in his hand. Tony figured that was to keep anyone from escaping. He sure wouldn't want to get whacked with a stick like that!

"Head straight on," Stilts instructed Chubbs, gesturing toward the Forbidden tunnel. "Once we're through this tunnel, we'll be there."

"You won't tell Mean-Eyed Max that I almost lost one of his new workers off the train tonight, will you?" Chubbs pleaded. "I didn't see the last man hiding in the very back of the baggage car, behind all the luggage and trunks. Mean-Eyed Max would be sore at me, if he ever found out."

"As long as you don't tell him that I only slipped the conductor half of what I was supposed to; he'll never know, and the conductor was happy getting what he got," Stilts added.

"I thought we were gonna share that extra money we saved from the conductor. I'll never tell," Chubbs vowed.

"Good," Stilts said. "We're partners."

"Yeah," Chubbs laughed, waving his stick. "Partners in crime! Get a move on up there, coolie! We ain't got all night."

The captives looked forlorn and scared as they were led away, their footsteps echoing softer and softer as they moved further into the tunnel. Tony felt sorry for them, but he'd learned something too. The workers were smuggled on the trains! And it sounded as if some of the conductors on the trains were taking bribes to keep quiet. Mean-Eyed Max seemed to have everything well thought out.

Tony waited to see if anyone else would come through the tunnels. The silence was oppressive. It weighed upon his ears until he could hear the hammering of his heart.

A huge lantern hanging from the ceiling flickered and caught his eye. What was it doing way up there? he wondered. That lantern was pretty useless up there, he decided. The light spilling from its core merely lit up the dirt ceiling in a small circumference that wouldn't do anyone any good. What a silly place to put a lantern. Only somebody really tall, like Stilts or Mean-Eyed Max could actually reach it to light it.

A foreign sound suddenly awakened Tony from his musings, and he realized that the steady noise had been going on for quite some time. His heart jumped into his throat. Someone was coming. The shuffling sound of footsteps echoed through the windy tunnel. They were coming from behind! He squeezed further into the small hole in the dirt wall, praying he was invisible. With the lack of light nearby, the tunnel travelers would only see the dark shadows where the crevice was located and with luck they would pass by without seeing him.

He pushed himself further into the minuscule space, wishing he was a mole. His heart thumped loudly as he pressed his face into the dirt wall, his nose touching the damp earth. Holding his breath, Tony willed himself invisible. It must have worked, for someone passed by without even hesitating.

Quietly pulling himself out of the indentation in the wall, he carefully poked his head around the dirt wall. "Hey! What are you doing down here?"

Tony jumped so high his head brushed the top of the tunnel, sending small chunks of earth raining down upon his shoulders. He'd been caught!

"These tunnels are my business too," a soft, calm voice answered. It was Mr. Wong!

Standing under the strange lantern were Mean-Eyed Max and Mr. Wong. They were arguing. The funny lantern shone on them and their faces glowed with a yellowish tinge.

"You better watch yourself, Wong," Mean-Eyed Max spat. "Leave my workers alone, if you know what's good for you! They're all indentured; there's nothing you can do for them. I don't keep illegal immigrants," he lied. "Come on, I'll prove it to you."

Suddenly Mean-Eyed Max reached up and tugged on the high lantern. It moved easily in his grasp. As it slid down on a thick chain, part of the dirt wall began to lift up. It rose like a garage door, as if hinged from the top. In amazement Tony stared as another tunnel became visible behind the hidden door.

Whoever had made this secret entrance was a genius! The door was actually made of thick wood. Dirt and gravel had been stuck to it and it was camouflaged against the rest of the tunnel. Tony watched as the men disappeared into the tunnel and the door began to lower as the lantern swung back toward the tunnel ceiling.

Don't go with him! Tony wanted to shout. Don't trust him! It could be an ambush! But Mr. Wong didn't seem to be afraid. Tony watched from his hiding spot as the men moved further into the tunnel. What should he do? Jumping out into the intersection, he hesitated. The dirt wall dropped closer to the ground right before Tony's eyes. Eddie was in there, he thought, remembering how he had disappeared so quickly that day. And Mr. Wong might need his help too. What if it was a trap? What if Mean-Eyed Max hurt Mr. Wong? It was all up to him!

Without conscious thought, Tony took a long running jump. Dropping to his stomach he slid under the door as if he were diving for home plate in a baseball game back home. The door was within centimetres of the ground and he felt his head brush against it as he slid underneath.

His backpack got caught on something and stopped him dead in his tracks. Panic spread like wildfire through his body. What if he got pinned to the ground by the door? It was probably heavy enough to crush his body! That horrible thought gave him an extra boost of adrenalin and he gave a mighty shove with the toes of his shoes. He felt something snap and he was free. Rolling quickly, he made it into the hidden tunnel just as the door touched the ground.

Breathing as if he'd just run a marathon, Tony lay curled up on the ground in the middle of the tunnel in the pitch dark waiting to be grabbed. Surely someone had heard all of the racket he'd just made! He lay in the darkness waiting for shouts of anger, trying to control his reckless breathing.

After a minute, he raised his head, his backpack jiggling as he moved. He hadn't attracted any attention, as far as he could tell. No one had come rushing back. He could hear Mean-Eyed Max and Mr. Wong shuffling through the tunnel not too far ahead of him, still arguing. Catching his breath, he stood up and cautiously began to follow at a discreet distance, ready at a moment's notice to help his new friend.

Arms outstretched, fingers just grazing both walls, he followed Mean-Eyed Max and Mr. Wong. He walked on rubbery legs, his heart beating wildly in his chest. He wasn't sure he was doing the right thing, but he knew he couldn't let Mr. Wong go on alone. They were so far ahead, their footsteps were fading, but he could still hear their angry voices floating on wind currents.

The backpack jolted with every step Tony took, his little key rings clinking as he walked. Reaching behind him, he tried grabbing them to keep them quiet. His hand grasped a cylindrical shape and Tony stifled a groan. In all the panic, he had forgotten that he had his penlight on a key ring! Pulling his backpack off his shoulders, Tony unclasped the flashlight and pushed the button. A small stream of light filled the tunnel, almost blinding him.

Inspecting the walls and ceiling, Tony gasped. This tunnel looked very dangerous and decrepit, the walls very rough. They looked like someone had hacked at them with a shovel. The ceiling wasn't much different, and from the mounds of dirt dotting the floor, Tony knew that several small cave-ins had already occurred. It looked like it wouldn't be long before a big one happened.

The tunnel seemed to go on forever, and Tony felt as if he was moving through space, or underwater. His movements were slow and awkward, and he wondered if he would be able to run fast if he had to. It felt as if the walls were closing in on him and he wanted to race back to the large and safer tunnel. But that would mean leaving Mr. Wong alone to fight Mean-Eyed Max and the other bad guys he was sure lurked in the tunnels. Resolutely, he continued. Maybe, he thought, he was a bit of a hero too.

Finally, when he felt as if he would go crazy in the underground void, Tony spotted a thin line of light ahead. It looked like a mirage; something he wanted so desperately that he was dreaming about it. As he moved toward it, he began to hear sounds and voices. Thumps and bumps came at regular intervals. There were several voices, some loud and demanding, others the quiet melodic sound of the Chinese language being spoken.

The tunnel divided, one part continuing in the dark earth. Tony turned toward the source of light. He found himself facing a flimsy door, slightly ajar. Light streamed from all sides of it, giving the door a surreal and radiant appearance. It reminded him of the door of an alien spaceship he had seen in a poster.

Tony snapped off his penlight, slipping it into his pocket. Wondering what to do, he stood beside the door for a moment. Then, gathering up his courage, he bravely leaned close and twisted his head this way and that, trying to catch a glimpse of what was on the other side. Having no luck, he sighed and then did the only thing left for him to do; he quietly pushed the door open a few centimetres further and slipped inside, pushing it closed behind him.

Once inside, Tony scooted away from the door and into a corner behind boxes and barrels. From this vantage point he watched, soon realizing he was in the basement of a grocery store. The thumps he'd heard were the sounds of wooden boxes being dropped to the floor or onto long wooden shelves or tables, which lined the dirt walls and marched in straight lines down the length of the basement.

Ripping sounds filled the air as paper was torn off the apples and other produce. Workers carried the heavy wooden boxes back and forth across the room. Some people washed and dried the food while others repacked it and carried it toward a set of steep wooden stairs. But where had Mean-Eyed Max and Mr. Wong gone? He hoped nothing terrible had happened to Mr. Wong.

For over half an hour, Tony watched the Chinese immigrants work, heaving the heavy boxes back and forth and carrying things up and down the stairs. A foreman walked back and forth, barking orders. He swung a long stick, shouting at the Chinese workers if they moved too slowly. Tony felt sorry for them. They probably couldn't understand English anyway, so why was this man wasting his breath?

Two young Chinese boys worked side by side, smiling and whispering to each other from time to time when the supervisor wasn't watching. They almost made it look like fun to be down here, as if they were actors in a movie about the tunnels. Tony took a closer look at them. Why, one of them was Eddie! Joy sluiced through his veins as he clamped both hands over his mouth to keep from calling out. He wiggled happily, feeling as if he was floating on the low ceiling of the basement. He'd found Eddie! He couldn't wait to tell the others.

Tony tried carefully attracting Eddie's attention by staring intently at him, hoping he would feel the vibes and look his way. He had to be cautious, though; he couldn't risk being caught here. But there was too much noise and confusion going on, and Eddie remained oblivious to his presence.

One worker finally went over and began to prepare some food, and Tony realized that it must be close to mealtime for them. He was confused. Checking his digital watch, he saw that it was close to 3:00 a.m., long past bedtime for most people. It was like these poor people had to work twenty-four hours a day!

Thinking carefully, he decided that when everyone sat down to eat he would make his escape. It was obvious that Mr. Wong was gone and it would be safer for Tony to leave too. The only other route out of the basement seemed to be the stairs. They were used so regularly that Tony knew he didn't have a hope of getting up them unnoticed unless everyone was busy doing something else. He would just have to bide his time, be patient. He couldn't wait to get back and tell the others. Wouldn't they be happy!

After what seemed like an eternity, the workers began to leave their jobs. They shuffled toward the table and sat down. Not wanting to waste any time, Tony crept out of his corner, trying to keep piles of boxes between him and the other people, especially the foreman, who seemed to have disappeared. He tried again, being bolder this time, to attract Eddie's attention, but had no success. His best bet was to get Andrea and Vance to help him rescue Eddie.

He skirted a wooden table a few metres from the stairs, and looking back, realized that he was home free. No one was paying the least attention to him; they didn't even know he was there! Relieved, he put one foot on the first step, knowing that he would soon be out of this horrible basement and back on the streets of Moose Jaw, breathing fresh, clean air.

"Hey, kid!" A booming voice caused Tony to jump so high his backpack almost flew off his shoulders. "I've been waiting for you."

A large, powerful hand grasped his shoulders and spun him around. "How'd you get down here with no one noticing?" Trying to breathe around the huge knot of fear which clogged his throat, Tony could only mouth the words; no sound came out.

"Never mind," the voice laughed. "That's a great skill to have in this business – sneaking in and out unnoticed. I thought Mean-Eyed Max said you were too chicken to come work for us. Guess you changed your mind, eh?" Looking Tony up and down he said, "You're a little on the scrawny side, but we'll fatten you up. You can eat with the coolies, if you can stomach their food!"

Confused, Tony tried to play along. "I-I'm not chicken." His voice squeaked and he noisily cleared his throat. "Wh-what's my job?"

"Name's Fred," the foreman said, sticking out his huge hand and engulfing Tony's, almost crushing it. "You're my gopher," he laughed again, but his eyes were cold, his lips curved into a sneer, and Tony shuddered. He didn't want a job working for this man, but he had no choice now.

"What's a gopher do?" Tony asked.

"You know, you 'go-fer' this and you 'go-fer' that..." He laughed again when he saw confusion clouding Tony's face. "What's your name?"

"Tony," he said, wondering too late if he should have given his real name.

"Well, Tony, you run errands, take messages, and sometimes take a coolie or two along and keep them in line. Think you can do it?"

Tony nodded confidently, although inside he was shaking with doubt. He wasn't sure what he was getting into, but he had to take the job. He didn't have much choice. How else could he explain why he was in the basement? At least it would be a way to stay close to Eddie, and maybe he could help Mr. Wong, wherever he was.

"I'll give you a little tour," Fred announced, pushing Tony toward the area where the coolies were busy eating. As they passed by the crowded table, Tony noticed that the thin soup they were wolfing down was grey and very watery. Bowls of rice were being consumed too. "Want some?" Fred asked, when he noticed Tony's keen interest.

Making a face, Tony quickly shook his head and looked away. "We just feed them enough to keep them alive," Fred informed him. "No need to waste good food on them. They're just coolies. Rice and gruel, that's all they get."

Sickened by what he had just heard, Tony fought to keep control of his emotions. He felt sad too. Why should people get treated so badly just because they were different? It didn't make any sense to him. These people were the indentured servants Andrea had been talking about. They were working long, hard hours for about twenty-five cents a day! Somebody was probably making a lot of money using them as cheap labour, he thought. He realized too, that by only feeding the Chinese workers poor quality food, the owner of the grocery store was making even more money.

"Now for your first job, Tony." Fred counted his workers and turned back. "Deliver this package to Mr. Maxwell."

"Who?" Tony asked, grasping a package about the size of a football to his chest.

Fred looked around nervously and then said softly, "Deliver it to Mean-Eyed Max, but don't ever let him hear you call him that."

Tony shivered, his knees turning to jelly. "Where do I find him?"

Fred led him to the doorway he had just entered and pointed down the tunnel in the opposite direction. "The tunnel gets kind of small, but you're a small fry, you should be fine. Mean-Eyed Max can do it bent over!"

"Here, let me put it in that suitcase you carry on your back; that'll keep your hands free," Fred offered, moving behind Tony to look for the opening.

"No!" Tony shouted, backing away. "I-I'll just carry it in my hands. It'll be okay." He didn't want Fred to find his hypodermic needles and insulin. How would he ever explain why he carried those things around with him? Without waiting for a response, he dove into the tunnel and away from Fred.

A Dangerous Mission

Tony travelled through the twisting tunnel, moving further and further away from the grocery store, wondering what he had gotten himself into. It sounded so dangerous.

The tunnel gave him the creeps too, making his skin crawl. It felt as skinny as a mole's hole and rough and bumpy besides. He almost fell several times, tripping over rocks embedded in the dirt floor. Feeling like a mole himself, he moved slowly through the winding mass of dirt and debris. This tunnel had an unfinished and uncared-for atmosphere, as if someone had quickly tunneled through the earth, meaning to get back and do a better job at some point, but never doing it.

Fred had said that he would easily find the place, but so far, Tony hadn't seen anything. Afraid to use his flashlight for fear someone might be coming from the other direction and notice it, he had to rely on the few lanterns suspended from posts. These often listed badly to one side, like the Leaning Tower of Pisa, and he worried they would fall over, bringing a huge load of dirt down with them.

The acrid smell of some kind of smoke reached Tony's nostrils. It didn't smell like cigarettes or cigars and he wondered what it could be. It had a sharp odour, so strong it burned in his nose. Turning the last curve in the tunnel, he came to a beaded curtain strung across an entranceway.

Bravely pushing the curtains aside, Tony stepped into a lounging area. The light was so dim everything was in shadow and he could barely see the wooden benches and planks stretched along the walls. The smoke was thicker in the small room. As his eyes adjusted to the darkness, he realized that several men lay on straw pallets on the floor or on wooden planks. They looked like rickety bunk beds without nice soft mattresses to lie on.

A strange looking contraption stood in the centre of the room. Long hoses came out of it, like the tentacles of an octopus. A man sucked on the end of a hose and he suddenly realized that the huge octopus was a smoking machine! Flickering candles dotted the area, making everything look supernatural. He felt as if he were in a strange underwater dream world.

Everyone seemed to move in slow motion, with dopey looks on their faces.

"What do you want?" an old man asked. From the deep shadows of the room, Tony could barely see him sitting in the far corner.

"Fred sent me to give this to Mean – I mean, Mr. Maxwell." Tony stumbled over the words, trying not to stare at anything too long. It was difficult. Everything looked so bizarre. He was in some kind of drug place. He wondered what his parents would think if they knew where he was. They'd be really angry, he decided, wishing they were here with him right now. He would take their anger over the terrible feelings this awful place was giving him.

"Hand it over," the old man said, reaching out to grab the package.

"No." Tony wrapped his arms around it and backed away. "I'm only supposed to give it to M-Mr. Maxwell.

The old man laughed, then shuffled over to another beaded partition and disappeared inside. The beads swayed, clinking together, adding to the fantastical atmosphere of the room.

Tony could hear groaning and moaning and then the curtains parted again and the old man reappeared with Mean-Eyed Max. Holding his breath, Tony handed over the package and began to back out of the room. He couldn't leave this awful place fast enough.

"Hey, don't I know you?" Mean-Eyed Max asked, his glass eye staring at Tony.

"I-I don't think so," Tony said, suddenly glad that it was so dark. He didn't want Mean-Eyed Max remembering him.

"Sure I do. You're the kid who was looking for a coolie for a friend!" He laughed. "You're better off sticking with those other kids I've seen you with. They your friends?" Reluctantly, Tony nodded, not sure how much information he should give away. He knew Mean-Eyed Max was not to be trusted.

"I've seen that tall fella and the younger girl around. Their dad's a cop. It pays to know these things." He flipped a coin in Tony's direction. "Your dad a cop?" Tony shook his head, hoping the questions were over. "You did a good job, boy. Tell Fred we'll keep you."

"Yes sir," he said as he stumbled out of the room. He leaned against the wall trying to calm his racing heart. That was a close call. Mean-Eyed Max knew way too much about all of them and that scared him.

What was all that stuff in there anyway? he wondered. Curiosity got the better of him and he turned back into the room, pushing the beads aside. "What do you call this stuff, anyway?"

"It's opium; made from poppies. It's good to smoke, sniff, or eat. It makes you feel good. Want to try some?" The old man smiled invitingly at Tony, his tone alluring. "The first time is always free."

The hairs on the back of Tony's neck stood up in alarm and he backed away, listening to his gut instincts. "No," he said firmly, just like he'd been taught to say in the Just Say No Club at school. What was opium, anyway? He had heard the word before, but he just couldn't remember much about it. "What is it?" he insisted.

"Something to make you feel good," the old man laughed again, shuffling toward Tony, a long hose in hand, stretched in Tony's direction.

"No way!" Tony stumbled, falling against the wall. Scrambling to his feet he fled down the tunnel, feeling as if the devil was on his tail.

"So you found it," Fred said, stepping in front of Tony as he entered the grocery area, practically slamming the door behind him. "You did a good job for such a small fella; you're fast too."

"Thanks," Tony smiled, trying to catch his breath. He was a mass of confusion and concern. "Who were those people at the opium den?" He blurted the question and then cringed, realizing that it was none of his business and he should have just kept his mouth shut.

Fred shrugged his shoulders. "They're workers. A few of them get hooked on the drug and spend a lot of their time there after work."

"Why do you let them go there?" Tony was suddenly angry with this man for his unconcerned attitude.

"The drug keeps them passive and under control," Fred replied. "They're happy like that."

Disgusted, Tony turned away. "What else do you want me to do?" he asked shortly.

Fred eyed him and looked as if he was going to call him on his rude behaviour, but changed his mind. "You're tired after your first night. Go home and get some rest. Come back tomorrow night around the same time. I always have jobs for a good worker like you, but remember, the work gets harder and the hours are long. Get some rest." Pulling his hand out of his pocket he dropped several coins into Tony's palm.

"Don't spend it all in one place," he joked.

"I won't." Pocketing the money, Tony felt guilt settle like a lump in the pit of his stomach. For one small job, he had just made double what the Chinese workers would make in a day! It was so unfair.

"I'll let you out of the door upstairs." Fred took the wooden steps two and three at a time, leaving Tony to traipse along behind him. They came to the landing, and he realized they were standing in a small closet area. Fred pushed open the door and they walked across the grocery store, skirting around wooden barrels full of pickles and other delights, and wooden shelves stocked with preserves. Light from the huge picture windows shone in from the street, engulfing much of the store in shadows so black that Fred disappeared entirely whenever he stepped into one.

At the door, Tony turned back to look down the long aisle. The light streaming in made it easy to read some of the product names closest to the door. A little bell tinkled and hit the glass as Fred opened the door. "Tomorrow then," he said, pushing Tony out and swiftly closing the door behind him. Tony heard the lock click into place. Fred disappeared into the shadows and was gone from sight.

WHERE'S MR. WONG?

Where am I? Tony wondered, glancing at the sign hanging above the door. It moved slightly as the wind blew, creaking as it swung on rusty hinges. "Wing's Grocery," he read, and he remembered the name from his earlier sighting of Eddie and his run-in with Mean-Eyed Max. Funny, the grocery store had a Chinese name, when it was obviously run by Mean-Eyed Max and his gang.

What had happened to Mr. Wong? he wondered. He hoped he wasn't in some kind of trouble.

Thinking he shouldn't be too far off Main Street, Tony trotted toward the corner, keeping in the shadows as much as possible. It wouldn't do, he knew, to be seen out this late at night alone. Only gangsters and bad guys hung out this late, and he didn't want to run into any of them. Hearing a noise behind him, he dove into the dark shadows cast by the nearby buildings and froze, holding his breath.

Footsteps marched swiftly up the street. They passed by, hesitating for a moment right where Tony was hidden. Holding his breath, his heart pounding in his ears, he closed his eyes, wishing he were safe at home, in the present, not here in olden days Moose Jaw, playing this dangerous game. A hand came down on his shoulder and he yelped in terror.

"Is that you, Tony?"

Tony came out of his hiding spot, relief written all over his face. "Boy, am I glad to see you, Mr. Wong! I followed you into the tunnels. I was worried Mean-Eyed Max might have hurt you!"

"Come with me," Mr. Wong said. "We need to make plans to rescue your friend, Eddie."

Mr. Wong led Tony to the back door of his café . He pushed the door open and called softly in Chinese. His wife appeared. Tony followed the Wongs into the living area of the building, past the room he had been in and into a smaller room.

The Wong family lived in cramped quarters at the back of the restaurant. It was even smaller than Rosie's suite, with a tiny kitchen and living room squashed together. It was small, but very clean. Two doors led off the living room and Tony assumed they were the bedrooms.

The couch had been hastily made up with sheets

and a blanket, and someone was lying on it. Mrs. Wong sighed and muttered in Chinese, her voice soft and comforting.

"What's wrong?" Tony asked.

"This person has been scalded by the hot water in the laundry," Mr. Wong translated. "It's very serious." Mrs. Wong spoke again, pointing to a shelf behind Tony's head. "Bring those jars of herbs and remedies, please," Mr. Wong instructed. "We can't call a doctor, but we have been trying to help this person."

Tony did as instructed, wondering what was in the jars. He watched as Mrs. Wong smeared something on the worker's neck and arms. Hearing the person moan, he turned away, the strong smell of the ointment filling his nostrils. Mr. Wong went into the kitchen and lit the stove. He placed a kettle over the flame. "I'm making a herbal tea remedy to take away the pain and help with the healing. This person will need much rest to get strong again."

"Now," Mr. Wong said, reaching on a high shelf to get a container of dried leaves, "you are brave, young Tony. Let us make plans to rescue your friend, Eddie."

WHERE'S BEANIE?

"Did everyone get enough sleep?" the mothering side of Rosie inquired the next morning as she stifled a big yawn. They sat around the kitchen table having breakfast. "I worry about all of you, tramping around in the dark and doing such dangerous things. Those tunnels are treacherous."

"Tony's still asleep," Andrea commented, glancing toward the closed bedroom door. She had just checked on him again. "I wonder why he's so tired?"

"He's usually the first one up," Beanie said, with suspicion. "I think he's been up to something."

"Like what?" Vance asked, helping himself to another piece of bread.

"Well, remember when we went for ice cream and we couldn't find him for a minute or two? How did

211

he get behind us like that?" Beanie asked.

"You think too much," Vance said.

"I went to look for the body, Andrea," Rosie continued, ignoring Vance and Beanie. "There was nothing there. I'm going to do some investigating. There's got to be a way for me to tell this story. The good citizens of Moose Jaw need to know what's going on here."

Everyone nodded in agreement and Andrea had to tell her story again. After she confessed to tripping over a body, the others wouldn't let her be until she had divulged all the details.

Tony sauntered into the kitchen. "Good morning," he grinned, glancing out the window to where the sun shone brightly. "It looks like another gorgeous day in Moose Jaw!"

"Just what have you been up to?" Beanie pounced. "You look as pleased as the cat who swallowed the canary."

"What?" Tony sputtered, realizing that his good humour had just given him away.

"Come on," Beanie said. "'Fess up! I know you've been up to something! I'll bet you snuck out last night!"

"Well," Andrea said sternly, her hands on her hips. "I have a feeling Beanie has guessed right about you! What were you doing last night?"

"I-I just got restless and took a little stroll," Tony hedged.

"Did this stroll include visiting the tunnels?" Vance asked.

Tony nodded, his eyes looking everywhere but at Andrea.

"Tony!" Andrea wailed. "You went there alone? But why? Don't you know how dangerous it could have been?"

"But I found Eddie!" Quickly, Tony recounted his tale of getting trapped in the tunnel, getting a job, and finding Eddie. Still, he kept silent about Mr. Wong and the burned worker.

"Wow!" Beanie enthused. "That's wonderful! You're a hero."

Vance grudgingly agreed. "You did well," he said, slapping Tony's shoulder.

Andrea still wasn't happy. "Next time you feel like a 'stroll' in the middle of the night, take one of us with you!"

"But how's Kami?" Tony asked, trying to get out of the hot seat. "I need to tell her my good news!"

"She's exhausted," Andrea answered. "She's sound asleep and has been that way for hours. We keep going in to check on her. I hope she's all right."

"I'm sure she'll sleep for a long time yet," Rosie reassured her. "After all, she's been through a horrible ordeal, poor girl. We'll let her sleep as long as she needs to."

"We'd better make sure she stays hidden here too.

She hasn't paid the Head Tax," Rosie reminded them. "Everyone will consider her an illegal immigrant."

Andrea's eyebrows disappeared under the rim of the hat. "That's right," she breathed, her eyes solemn. "Kami could be in big trouble if she's seen outside."

"What can you tell me about Wing's Grocery, where you think your friend, Eddie is being held captive? Where is that secret tunnel located, Tony?" Rosie asked.

Everyone watched while Tony drew the tunnel, explaining where he thought it was located. He explained how well it was camouflaged, and how the lantern hanging near the ceiling had to be pulled in order to get the tunnel door open. "It's on a pulley of some kind."

"I am worried about Eddie." Tony suddenly remembered, "There's a drug down there too. O-opi –"

"Opium?" Andrea questioned, her heart lurching. "We need to rescue him as soon as possible! We don't want him near that kind of stuff!"

Nodding, Tony explained, "There's some kind of drug den near there, run by Mean-Eyed Max and his gang. It's a scary, dangerous place. But it's more than that," he added, remembering something Mr. Wong had said. "I think Mean-Eyed Max and his gang are buying and selling opium and smuggling it around in the fruit crates the Chinese workers are packing up."

"Why do you think that?" Rosie asked, already thinking of another great news scoop.

Tony shrugged his shoulders, still not certain he should mention Mr. Wong. "I just do. I saw strange things going on when I was down there. There are an awful lot of workers there – more than a small grocery store would need. And why did I have to take a package to that opium den? It seemed just the right size to be drugs."

Studying the map Tony had drawn, Vance decided, "We'll go through this end of the tunnel, where Tony went in. We'll do it very early tomorrow morning, say four o'clock. Andrea and I will do this," he said firmly amid protests from the other two. "This could be really dangerous. We may need you, though, Tony," he added, "since you know the supervisor. We may need you to go in and distract him somehow."

"But that means that I'll need to go to work tonight, again!" Tony tried to keep the excitement out of his voice.

"No!" Andrea stamped her foot. "It's way too dangerous!"

"I have to, Andrea. I could meet you at the tunnel entrance when the coast is clear and lead you there!" Enthusiasm rang in his voice as he thought of all the possibilities. "It all makes sense."

Sighing, Andrea had to reluctantly agree. "We need Tony in on this one, Vance."

"What about me?" Beanie demanded, but Vance gave her a stinging glance. "I always miss the fun parts!"

215

So it was agreed that Tony would report back for work at Wing's Grocery that night. Andrea and Vance would go into the tunnel and wait – this was the most dangerous part, for they hadn't figured out where they could hide. When the coast was clear, at four in the morning, Tony would tap a secret knock on the wall and Andrea and Vance would open the tunnel door. They would grab Eddie and escape.

"That's a good plan," Beanie admitted, even though she wasn't involved. "It's so simple, it has to work!"

"What's going on?" Kami asked from the doorway. She stood stretching, reaching her fingers toward the high ceiling.

"We're trying to figure out how to rescue Eddie," Andrea said.

"I want to help!" Kami was instantly awake. "After all, he's *my* brother and I know the kind of trouble he's in!"

"You can't help," Vance reminded her gently. "You have to stay hidden."

"Why?" Kami demanded, flouncing over to Vance's side.

"Because you haven't paid the Head Tax. Everyone will think you're an illegal immigrant."

"Right," Kami said, suddenly feeling deflated. "I forgot about that. I'm a prisoner, right here in Canada! Can you believe it? I can't even walk down the street in my own country without getting arrested and deported, just because I look different than all of you. I feel —" she searched for the word, blinking back tears of frustration. "I feel degraded, like I'm less important than you."

"But we don't feel that way about you," Andrea said, trying to comfort her. "Thank goodness things have changed for the better in our time."

"Yes," Kami replied, still upset. "But how can I help? How can I be of use when I can't go outside?"

"You can help me take care of Baby Alan," Rosie cut in smoothly. "It looks like he's taking a shine to you."

Kami looked down. Baby Alan was toddling toward her, his arms reaching out. "Aw-w-w," she said, bending down to scoop him up, forcing the sad thoughts away. "We'll have fun together, won't we?"

"You can go read him a story," Rosie suggested. "He can have a nap."

"Okay," Kami agreed, taking the baby into the bedroom. "And then I think I'll hit the sack again. I'm still really tired. See you." She shut the door behind them.

THIS IS A RAID!

Tony returned to Wing's Grocery, through the front door this time, and was greeted cordially and put right to work. He ran a few errands around town, delivering boxes of what looked to be groceries. Curiosity finally got the better of him, and he stopped in the shadows of a side street to search a box. Moving fruit and other groceries around, his hands encountered a small sack. Was this how they smuggled the opium?

Repacking the box, Tony hurried to the address, finding himself at a scary-looking apartment building at the far end of River Street. The lights had been knocked out and several of the windows were cracked and broken. A piece of torn curtain hung outside one window, flapping against the bricks. He double-checked the address to make sure he was at the right place. It didn't look like anyone would live here!

"Hey!" a voice called out. "Up here! I've been waiting for you! Have you got my stuff?"

"Yes, I've got your grocery order," Tony replied, hoping the man would come down to get it. He didn't like the idea of going into this awful looking building.

"It's not the groceries I care about," the man replied. "It's the other stuff in there that I want!" He moved away from the window and Tony heard a door bang open, slamming against a wall. Good, he was coming downstairs.

The outside door was flung open and the man grabbed the box out of Tony's hands and dumped it on the step. Pushing apples and other things aside, he quickly found the little cloth sack. "Thanks," he said, flipping a coin in Tony's direction. He stepped over the groceries, leaving them strewn around the door, forgotten. "See you next time."

I hope not, Tony thought, looking at the food going to waste. There was nothing he could do about it. But now he knew the truth. It was opium he was carrying, and that scared him just thinking about it.

Tony ran many of these kinds of errands all evening and into the late night. Each time he returned and entered the basement area, he looked carefully at each worker, hoping to spot Eddie. The plan to rescue Eddie would only work if he could find him. Where could he be? It was as if Eddie had disappeared!

Finally back in the basement of the grocery store again after his last delivery, Tony sat down in a far corner to have a quiet, well-deserved break. Hidden behind tall boxes, barrels shielding him from sight, he stared out at the workers, still hoping to catch a glimpse of Eddie.

Watching the workers carefully, Tony nibbled on a piece of cheese he had grabbed from Rosie's and wrapped in a piece of cloth. There, over in the corner sorting fruit. Was that Eddie? No, Tony sighed, he was too tall. There! Stirring the soup on the stove; that had to be Eddie. No, he was too thin. There! Sitting at the table, eating. Was that Eddie? Carefully observing the worker, his eyes narrowed in concentration, Tony followed his every movement. As he got up from the table, the light momentarily lit his face. Tony realized joyfully that it was Eddie!

Grinning with relief, Tony wolfed down the cheese and began forming a plan. He would wait until they had all gone to bed for the night, then he would grab Eddie and make a run down the tunnel. By that time Vance and Andrea would be there and would open the hidden entrance. They would probably use the Forbidden tunnel and head back to Rosie's via the tunnel system; that would likely be the safest and fastest way to go. It was an excellent plan, even if he did say so himself.

Pleased as punch that things were going so well, Tony relaxed in his corner, almost falling asleep. After all, he decided, the foreman didn't need him, and he wanted to be alert and ready when the time came for putting his plan into action.

"I think I'll go home now," Beanie announced, yawning widely and stretching her arms high over her head in a dramatic manner. "I'm really tired." Watching Tony proudly don his backpack and head out the door for his job had made her mad. She wanted part of the action too.

Andrea felt a sense of uneasiness settle in the pit of her stomach. "I'll be glad when this night is over and we have Tony and Eddie safely with us," she said as she and Sarah washed dishes.

"Me too," Vance said from across the room. He eyed Beanie suspiciously as she prepared to leave. "Make sure you do go straight home," he ordered. "Or maybe I should walk you home."

"No," Beanie said, hurrying toward the door. "I'll be all right."

Slipping down the stairs, she ran out into the night, hurrying down Ominica Street toward Main. Annoyed that Tony was getting all of the excitement this time, she was bound and determined to find her part in this adventure. She was just as capable as any boy of taking care of herself! Vance should know that by now.

Travelling down Main Street, Beanie was careful to stay in the shadows of the buildings. It was so quiet tonight; unusually so, she thought, gazing down the street. It felt as if something was about to happen. She could see the lit face of the post office clock a block south, where it stood on a high tower overlooking the downtown. Why was she the only person on the street? she wondered. Studying the clock, she realized it was after midnight.

Suddenly a car went whizzing past, all of its lights off. It careened around the corner ahead, heading west on River Street. Wondering what all the excitement was, Beanie followed it. Soon another car wheeled around the same corner and she recognized it as one of the town's police cars. Something big must be happening! Forgetting to stay in the shadows, she approached the corner at a run.

Peeking around the building, Beanie watched as several silhouetted figures erupted from the cars, heading for a building on the north side of the street. Listening hard, Beanie heard the unmistakable sound of breaking glass and the loud bang of the door being kicked open.

"This is a raid!"

TONY was in such a stupor that the sounds overhead had been going on for quite some time before he became aware of them: a sharp bang and then the tinkle of glass breaking, followed by strange scuffling noises.

There was sudden and loud pounding on the floor and then he heard the unmistakable words: "This is a raid!" Loud crashing sounds came from upstairs as the policemen ran around knocking over shelves and throwing open doors, looking for the bad guys.

"Here, take this, kid," Fred yelled, pushing a heavy cloth sack into Tony's backpack as he glanced nervously toward the stairs. "Mean-Eyed Max told me that if anything like this ever happened, I was to give the sack to the tunnel runner, and that's you. He'll come looking for you, and for this, so keep it safe, if you know what's good for you. And don't skip town, kid, or your neck will be in a noose, got that?"

Tony nodded numbly at the threatening sound of Fred's voice. "Now I'm getting out of here. You're on your own, kid. A small kid like you can find a good hiding place until the heat is off. Try over there." He pointed at a mass of boxes strewn about the area and then took off.

Stumbling over cases and tables, Tony managed to find the hiding place. He wedged himself against the wall, surrounded by the tables and cases. He hoped no one would find him.

The door leading into the basement was flung open and many pairs of boots pounded down the stairs. Suddenly the room was filled with policemen yelling, brandishing guns and sticks. Everyone froze for a second, and then pandemonium ensued with people running in all directions trying to escape.

From his vantage point, Tony watched Fred race toward the tunnel entrance at the far end of the basement. A policeman grabbed him as he tried to run past and pushed him to the ground, calling for help as he did so.

Within a minute, Fred was escorted up the stairs, arrested. As he was led past Tony's hiding place, he turned his head, making eye contact with him. Then Tony saw his lips form the words, "Mean-Eyed Max." Shuddering, he wondered what was so important that Mean-Eyed Max would come after it.

Tony sat frozen to the ground, watching everything unfold right before his eyes. Chaos abounded as the police dragged the immigrants up the stairs. He watched, his heart in his stomach, as Eddie was dragged, kicking and squirming, up the stairs and out of view. Eddie had been arrested!

It seemed like an eternity before the basement grew quiet. Silence drummed in Tony's ears as he sat in the dark wondering if he was alone, listening for any sound that would indicate he had unwanted company. All he heard was his own heart pounding in his chest.

Finally, curiosity and fear got the best of him. Reaching for his backpack, he found his flashlight and switched it on.

The basement looked like a tornado had hit it. Tables were overturned, fruit spilled all over the floor. Barrels and boxes were tipped on their sides. It was an incredible mess. But at least he seemed to be alone.

Tony stood up, stretching his cramped muscles, and tried to pick up his backpack. It weighed a ton! What had Fred stuck inside? Carefully, he rooted around and found the bag. He untied the knot, opened it, and shone his light inside. Dazzling light bounced back in his face, almost blinding him, and he knew for certain why Mean-Eyed Max would be looking for him. He was carrying what felt like a ton of money; paper bills and coins. Mean-Eyed Max would want his money soon.

Terrified, Tony realized that he couldn't just climb the stairs and leave by the front door. The police probably had the place under surveillance and Mean-Eyed Max was most likely waiting for him too. His best bet was to go into that scary tunnel and wait for Andrea and Vance, as they had planned. He would go now, since Mean-Eyed Max would probably be too afraid to come looking for him quite so soon. That would give Tony the chance to try to find a small hole or crack in the tunnel to hide in. If Mean-Eyed Max came along first, this would be his only chance.

Carefully, he retied the bag and stuffed it into his backpack. He moved stealthily from his hiding spot, the beam from the flashlight bouncing as he walked. Suddenly the flashlight was snatched from his hand and he found himself staring into its blinding light, but not before he noticed a long black coat, bright smile, and derby hat.

Bubbling over with excitement, Beanie moved further down the street, toward the commotion. She didn't want to miss any of the action. Soon, the police would bring the bad guys out and load them into the waiting cars to be taken to the station. Maybe there would be a shoot-out right in Moose Jaw! She decided to stick around and watch it all. At least she would have impressive stories of spine-tingling danger to share with everyone.

The first of the men were brought out to the cars, distracting her further. Even in the dark, she could see that they were Chinese immigrants! What had they done wrong? she wondered. Then she remembered. The men working and living in the tunnels were in Canada illegally. What would happen to them? Would they be sent back to China?

The wind picked up again and set a sign swaying, nudging her faulty memory into action. "Wing's Grocery," she moaned aloud. Tony was in there and he was in danger! He might even get arrested!

Whirling around to race back to Rosie's with the terrifying news, Beanie collided with a hard object. It sent her plunging to the dark sidewalk on her hands and knees. "Ow-w-w!" she cried, rubbing her hands together, feeling them sting. She had skinned both her hands and knees in the fall.

Rough hands reached to grab her, one slapping itself over her mouth. She was dragged around the corner and onto Main Street, pulled into a dark shadowy space between buildings. "What's your hurry, kid?" a loud voice sneered, and Beanie trembled uncontrollably. She recognized the sinister voice of Mean-Eyed Max.

Mean-Eyed Max picked Beanie up like a sack of potatoes and flung her over his shoulder, carrying her briskly down the street.

"Scream, girlie, and you're done for," he said, his voice deadly quiet, and she knew he was serious. "You're not my tunnel runner, but he's a friend of yours. I saw you two together. You seem to be on friendly terms with that nosy newspaper dame too. I don't like nosy news reporters. By now I'm pretty sure that tunnel runner has something of mine, and now I have something of his – you," he laughed a sinister laugh and terror gripped Beanie's heart. "You're mine until he forks over my property. I'm sure he wouldn't keep it. You're just a precaution, in case he gets any funny ideas."

Riding high above the ground, bouncing with every step Max took, Beanie wondered where he was taking her. No one knew where she was. Terror lodged in her throat and she gulped air, trying to keep her wits about her and her mind clear. This was the worst danger she had ever been in. She was afraid to think about what would happen next.

MEAN-EYED MAX GETS NASTY

Footsteps thundered up the stairs and a loud knock sounded on Rosie's door. "There's been a raid!" a man's voice called through the door. Too impatient to wait for it to open, he turned the knob and rushed into the kitchen. It was Mr. Smith, the owner of the newspaper. "I'm heading over to the police station with the camera. Come along, my dear," he ordered. "We need to get this story for the morning paper! Looks like we'll be up all night!"

"Where was the raid?" Vance asked, as Rosie searched for her notebook.

"A little Chinese grocery store on High Street." Mr. Smith shook his head. "It looked so innocent to me, but it seems they had many illegal immigrants working as indentured labour and hiding in the basement."

Listening in, Andrea felt the hairs on the back of her neck stand up in alarm. "What was the name of it?" she asked, the words tumbling over themselves in her haste to speak them.

Mr. Smith checked his notes. "Wing's Grocery," he called over his shoulder as he raced down the stairs again. "Get to the police station fast, Rosie! We don't want to miss anything."

"Oh no," Andrea moaned as her head whirled in fear. "Where's Tony? What's happened to Tony?" Suddenly a thought jumped into her head.

"I guess the police aren't corrupt, after all," Andrea said with a groan. "But why did they have to choose Wing's Grocery to start with?" She madly paced the floor, pivoting swiftly on her heels at each wall and pacing back again. "Why couldn't they have chosen the warehouse? Why is everything going wrong?" she wailed, throwing her arms into the air in frustration.

"Take it easy," Vance said.

"What's going to happen to my little brother?" Andrea cried. "Will they arrest him? What if they put him in jail? What if we never get back to the future?"

"Don't even think about that," Rosie admonished, worry making her voice sound harsh. "Try to stay calm, Andrea," she said, putting her arms around the distraught girl. "Stay with her, Sarah. I'll go see if I can find out what happened to Tony." Sarah nodded, her mouth set in a grim, tense line.

"No," Andrea protested. "I'm coming with you. I have to find out what happened to Tony."

"You're too upset, Andrea," Sarah comforted. "Stay here with me."

Wiping the tears away with her shirtsleeve, Andrea finger-combed her short hair into place and jammed the cap on her head. "I'm ready now and in control. I can do this, and besides," she continued as everyone looked dubious, "I'm the only one who can identify Eddie. He's probably in jail."

"You're right," Rosie conceded. "Come on then."

"I'm coming with you," Vance said, grabbing his hat and slapping it on his head. "I don't want you two wandering around with gangsters on the loose." Taking Rosie's arm, he escorted her out of the room. Andrea followed along behind, pulling the door closed behind them.

The trip to the police station was a huge blur in Andrea's mind. Voices yelling and screaming, some calling out in other languages, assaulted her ears. Police officers gave up trying to get order and peace, hurriedly filling out papers and taking prisoners away.

There were so many under arrest that Andrea wondered if they would all fit in the cells. Rosie, on the pretense of interviewing the constables as they worked, asked if they had arrested any young boys and was told that the illegal immigrants were all in their teens. Not satisfied, she insisted on being escorted

– with Andrea – past the cells where the Chinese workers stood shoulder to shoulder, since it was too crowded to sit down.

"What will they do with them?" Andrea asked as they neared the end of the tour, having seen neither boy.

"I think I heard one officer say that they each had to come up with the Head Tax or get deported back to China." Rosie sighed. "Things are so bad there, it's too bad we can't find a way to keep these people."

Looking in at the sea of faces, at olive skin and glossy black hair, Andrea felt very sorry for the workers. They were treated badly in Canada, but going back to China would be no picnic either. A face, familiar, caught her attention and she stopped in her tracks. "There's Eddie," she shouted, pointing excitedly to a young man standing in the corner at the very back of the cell. She had almost missed seeing him, he was so far away, almost lost in the sea of humanity.

"At least we know where he is," Vance said. "I just don't know how we'll get him out of here."

"We'll think of something," Rosie said, making wild slashes of writing across her notebook. "There's so much information here, I could write stories for a whole month!"

"Now we just have to find Tony," Andrea said, scanning the crowd and relieved not to find him. "He's not here."

"That's good and bad," Vance replied, scratching his head. "I wonder where he is?"

Coming to an abrupt stop Andrea spun around. "Hiding! Hiding! That's why Tony's not here," she said, conviction strong in her voice. "I can feel it. He heard them coming and he's hiding! He's waiting for us to come and get him out of the hidden tunnel, just like we planned! We'd better go look for him now."

Anticipating Andrea's actions, Rosie clutched her arm to keep her from running away. "I'm not done here yet, but you two go ahead. Mr. Smith is still over there taking photographs. Good luck finding Tony."

"Let's go now, Vance," Andrea begged, pushing her way through the milling crowd toward the door. Vance followed in her wake.

The cool night air greeted them as they stepped outside the doors. "Whew, I'm glad to be out of that. What a jumble of confusion and noise! It's a mess in there!"

"Yes," Vance agreed absently, his eyes scanning the shadows across the street. "I think I just saw something move over there," he said, deliberately keeping his voice low. "Don't look," he cautioned Andrea when she made a move to do so. "It's a person. We don't want him to know we're on to him."

"But who would be following us?"

"I don't know." His voice sounded worried and he took her hand in his. "Don't run, but walk fast and act natural. We'll head to Rosie's place for now. Maybe we'll be able to lose him before we get there." Tugging at her hand, Vance walked on purposefully.

"Hey, Vance!" a voice called out of the darkness.

"That's Jack," Andrea realized, pulling her hand away and turning back. "We don't need to be afraid of him."

Looking doubtful, Vance stopped and waited while Jack approached from the shadows across the street. "I don't think he's alone," he muttered, keeping his voice low. "If trouble starts, you run back to the police station and get help."

Jack caught up to them, a smile pasted on his face. "Good evening!" he greeted loudly. It sounded phony to Andrea's ears. "How are you two?"

"F-fine," Andrea replied, staring at Jack. "Are you okay?"

"No, and neither are you two," he whispered, his lips barely moving. "I'm here to deliver a message from Mean-Eyed Max. He's got your little sister, Vance, and he intends to keep her until you hand over his property."

"What?" Andrea yelled, feeling the world begin to spin as she digested this horrible news. "Not Beanie too!" She felt as if she was going to faint.

"Beanie?" Vance's mouth sagged open in disbelief. "Where is she?"

"I don't know," Jack answered, but his eyes darted

over Vance's head and into the night, and Andrea wondered if he was telling the truth.

"What property do we have that belongs to Mean-Eyed Max?" Andrea wondered, racking her brain to figure things out. "We haven't kept any laundry and we didn't steal anything when we were in the warehouse."

Suddenly, Mean-Eyed Max was upon them, having snuck up while they listened to Jack. His large hands squeezed their necks in painful grips. "That tunnel runner has my property and I want it back," he rasped, his lips so close to Andrea's ear she could feel moisture on her cheek. "Give me my property and you get the kid. You have twenty-four hours before I do some damage to her. And don't you tell that cop father of yours," he cautioned Vance, "or anyone else!""

A police car turned the corner and the gangster disappeared into the shadows again as silently as he had appeared. "He means Tony," Andrea whispered, her voice hollow with terror. "He thinks Tony has something that belongs to him."

"I'm going after him," Vance turned on his heel, stalking after Mean-Eyed Max, his fingers clenched into tight fists of horror. "I'm not letting him get away with this!"

"I'm coming too," Jack called out. "I'm on your side, Vance. I'll do whatever I can to help."

"But what about Tony?" Andrea called as the night

wrapped cool fingers of fear around her.

"I'll meet you at Rosie's in five minutes," Vance yelled over his shoulder. "I'll be back as soon as I figure out where Beanie is and what Mean-Eyed Max is really up to. Then we can go find Tony. And Andrea, don't tell anybody – not even Rosie!"

A Tunnel Rat?

A ndrea stood staring into the dark where the boys had disappeared, her eyes brimming with tears. This was getting to be more than she could bear. She just wanted to go home to the present where she wouldn't have to worry about bad men and saving Eddie, Tony, and now Beanie! Panic eating away at her insides, she headed for Rosie's at a run. It was times like this she wished she had the convenience of a cellphone.

How absurd Vance was, she thought. No, just panicked and scared, she corrected herself. He was worried sick about Beanie and so was she. If only he hadn't been so foolish, chasing after Mean-Eyed Max like that. Max was a dangerous man. What if Vance got hurt? Or worse yet, kidnapped too? She blocked those awful thoughts from her mind as she flew up the stairs, already counting down the minutes until Vance would arrive.

"I CAN'T WAIT ANY LONGER," Andrea told Sarah and Rosie. "Vance was supposed to meet me here ten minutes ago. Where is he?!" She paced from the window to the door and back again in a tight circle, goosebumps standing out on her forearms.

"It's almost morning and Tony needs food once he takes his insulin. He's got the insulin with him, I hope, but he can't take it until he has food to eat afterward, and I know he was running low on snacks and things."

"Otherwise he'll have another one of those attacks like last time," Rosie remembered. "It was an awful shock having him carried into the house like that."

"It's scary for Tony too," Andrea said, preparing to leave. "I have to find him fast. I know where that huge lantern is that Tony talked about. I'm sure he's in that hidden tunnel waiting for us. If I don't come, he'll get really worried. I have to go find him."

"I'm coming too," Sarah declared, her voice firm and certain.

"You can't," both Rosie and Andrea gasped.

"You're a – a –" Andrea stumbled over the words, smiling. "I was going to say, you're a girl, but that doesn't make sense!"

"You mean, I'm a prim and proper lady who doesn't get her hands dirty with such things."

Blushing and avoiding Sarah's eyes, Andrea nodded. "I – I didn't mean it badly, Sarah."

"I know. The truth is, I've been curious about those tunnels and...and you need help. You can't go in there alone. Something terrible could happen to you too!"

Nodding, Andrea sighed with relief. "I really didn't want to go back there alone, Sarah. I'd be grateful for your help."

"You can't wear that into the tunnels," Rosie declared, ruefully eyeing Sarah's pretty blue dress. "You'd never be able to run. It's a good thing Andrea had to borrow more of Vance's clothes, since she's been here so long."

Sarah nodded, dashing into the bedroom. "I'll be right back."

Waiting, Andrea paced the room, impatient to find Tony and desperately terrified of what was happening to Beanie. Her mind kept flip-flopping from one crisis to the other until she felt almost crazy with worry. She wished she could tell Rosie about Beanie, but Vance had asked her not to.

Tony's tormented face was seared into her mind as she imagined the relentless sound of a time bomb ticking toward disaster. He was in grave danger and she had to find him fast. Then they would figure out what to do about Beanie.

It felt like an eternity, but was only a matter of minutes, before Sarah returned. "Well, how do I look?" she asked shyly, turning around in the middle of the kitchen for inspection. She was wearing Vance's extra overalls, cinched up to keep the shoulder straps in place. A huge work shirt was stuffed into the waist, bulging slightly.

Andrea grinned. "You look great." Leaning over, she gave Sarah a huge hug. "Thanks for helping me. Here, wear the cap. You need it more than I do!"

"I just want to help you find Tony. I'm worried about him too," Sarah said as she stuffed her hair up under the cap. "There. I'm ready to go."

"Be careful, and good luck," Rosie called to them as she handed Sarah a cloth sack containing food for Tony. The girls hurried down the stairs and headed to the Hazelton Hotel. There they entered the side entrance, creeping down the dilapidated staircase and into the tunnels.

"Oh," Sarah gasped, gripping Andrea's clothes, "these tunnels are as awful as you said. How do you stand it down here?"

"You do get used to it," Andrea said grimly, moving ahead into the Windy tunnel. "Stick close to me so you don't get lost."

"Don't worry," Sarah muttered between clenched teeth. "I've got a death grip on your shirt."

Travelling silently, trying hard not to scuffle their

feet, they listened for any sound that would indicate that they were not alone. The tunnel was as suffocating as Andrea remembered, and she wondered how Sarah was feeling. Brave trooper that she was, she hadn't yet complained or demanded to be taken back.

Claustrophobia rose up, bringing the tunnel walls closer and closer together until Andrea was sure she wouldn't be able to stand it one second longer. Bravely they pushed on. At last they reached the Main Street tunnel and stopped for a moment. "How are you doing, Sarah?" Andrea asked, studying her pale face under the light of a lantern. She wondered if she had made a mistake in bringing Sarah down here.

"I-I'm fine," Sarah stuttered, white with fear. "It is safe under the earth like this?" she couldn't help asking.

"I wouldn't call it super safe," Andrea said. "You wouldn't want to spend a lot of time down here."

"What do we do if we run into other people?" Sarah asked, not sure she wanted to know the answer.

"Run and try to find a place to hide," Andrea said, indicating one of the few narrow places where one could squeeze into the dirt wall. "But I don't think, with the raids happening, that anyone else will be down here. I think luck is on our side for a change." They kept walking.

"There's the lantern," Andrea pointed excitedly as they stepped out of the Main Street tunnel. "We need to pull down on that." Standing on tiptoe, she found she could just reach it.

The steady sound of gravel crunching caught Andrea's attention. "Oh no! Someone's coming!" Now voices could be heard from the direction of the train station.

"Quick!" Sarah hissed. "Do something!"

"Pull!" Andrea pleaded, stretching up to reach for the lantern and rope. "Pull the lantern!" Together they grabbed the chain and pulled. Slowly the door inched up. "It's too heavy, I can't do it..."

A muffled cry was heard and Andrea felt something grab her around the legs. "Tony!" she cried, almost releasing the lantern in surprise. Wriggling under the door, Tony lay on the dirt floor gasping in relief. Releasing the lantern, Andrea grabbed her brother in a big bear hug, swinging him up off the ground and around in a circle of delight.

"Come on," Sarah said, taking charge. "We've got to get out of here!"

Grabbing at one another for support, they fled into the Forbidden tunnel, not caring how much noise they made. They tripped over their feet in order to stay close together, stumbling and nearly falling in the process. Passing one of the lanterns, Andrea whipped it off its stand, taking it with them. "Now we can see where we're going," she said, turning up the flame and holding it high so that the light shone around them.

"We can go faster this way."

As they neared the end of the tunnel, Tony began to stumble and fell to his knees. "I can't go on," he gasped. "I missed..."

The sounds were still audible, although Andrea wasn't certain they had been followed into the Forbidden tunnel. "We'll hide here, in the storage area," she said, leading the others into the far corner, away from the light and usual traffic spots. "I think we'll be safe here."

"I missed my last shot of insulin," Tony wheezed. "I'm so thirsty."

Setting the lantern on the ground, Andrea whipped Tony's backpack off his back and unzipped it. She pulled out a juice box and he started to dink. Rummaging around, she found the syringe, with its protective tip, the insulin bottle, and an alcohol wipe. With shaky hands, she pushed the tip of the needle into the insulin bottle, trying to remember the last time she had done this for Tony. It had been too long. She hoped she remembered what to do.

The voices and footsteps continued to grow louder. "They're coming through the Forbidden tunnel," Sarah reported her eyes huge with terror. Spotting the bright lantern, she grabbed it. "Hurry, Andrea! We have to put this out now or we'll be caught!"

Rolling up Tony's pant leg, Andrea concentrated, blinking sweat out of her eyes. She ripped the foil package off the alcohol pad and swabbed his leg. Needle in hand, she held her breath and stuck it in, pushing the plunger and counting slowly to ten. "There, all done." They were suddenly thrown into darkness as Sarah extinguished the lantern.

Two men, one carrying a lantern, entered the underground storage area as the kids sat frozen in the corner. Andrea recognized Mean-Eyed Max and Chubbs.

"How could you lose a body?" Mean-Eyed Max roared. "No one loses a body!"

"I don't think the coolie was dead, s-sir," Chubbs sputtered.

"Well, you could have taken care of that too! And now the body has disappeared and we're in big trouble!"

"I-I'm not a killer," Chubbs admitted, wringing his hands.

"That's why you're not the boss." Mean-Eyed Max jabbed a finger in Chubbs' chest. "You're too soft."

"I didn't leave the body there for long —"

"No, just long enough for it to disappear, that's all!" Mean-Eyed Max took a swing at Chubbs, who ducked, backing away.

"I was just going to get the truck, Boss, and then it wouldn't start. I hate these new-fangled inventions! Why can't we go back to the horse and buggy? At least the horse is always ready to go!"

Mean-Eyed Max took another swing at Chubbs and missed entirely. He calmed down a bit, his anger spent. "I've got another job for you and you better not mess up on it." He waved a threatening fist under Chubbs's nose.

"I kidnapped that snoopy kid. She's hidden in the tunnels a ways back. You feed her – just enough to keep her alive, mind, and nothing more. Her big brother better come through with my property or she's one dead duck!"

"You can't get into killing kids," Chubbs admonished. Realizing his mistake, he began to back away from Mean-Eyed Max. He made a break for it and hightailed it toward the warehouse door at the far end of the underground storage area.

"Get back here," Mean-Eyed Max yelled, chasing after him. "I'm not done with you yet!" He tripped along after Chubbs, reaching the door and half falling into the warehouse as he raced up the steps.

The door slammed, leaving the three in total silence and darkness, relief washing over them. "Here, Tony," Sarah suddenly remembered. "Turn on your flashlight. Here's some food."

Tony turned on his flashlight, then opened the sack and began to eat. "Who do you think he kidnapped?" he asked between huge bites of bread.

"They've got Beanie," Andrea answered, tears brimming, her voice tight. "We've got to find her fast."

"Beanie?!" both Sarah and Tony gasped.

"But why would they take Beanie?" Tony wondered, totally baffled. "She hasn't done anything."

"It sounds like they think you have something of theirs – something Mean-Eyed Max wants," Sarah said.

"I do," Tony grabbed his backpack and began fishing something out of it. Eyes huge and voice solemn, Tony opened the cloth sack. "I have all this money, Andrea. No wonder Mean-Eyed Max kidnapped Beanie. He wants his money back." They sat quietly for a long time, wondering if the bad guys would come back. Suddenly more scuffling noises were heard coming from the direction of the Forbidden Tunnel. "Oh no," Andrea moaned. "Not more trouble." Tony flipped off his flashlight.

"Sh-h-h," Sarah warned. Searching the ground she found a piece of wood from a broken crate. "I'll protect us!" She stood, moving as silently as a shadow toward the other side of the storage area. She reached the entrance to the far tunnel just as the other person stepped into the underground cavern. Without a thought, Sarah swung the stick, the blow glancing off the person's shoulder.

"Ow-w-w!" a male voice cried, hands reaching up to stop the blows.

"Get out of here," Sarah yelled, raining blows down upon the person's shoulders and head. "Get out, I said."

The hands stilled as the head turned toward the voice. "Sarah?"

"Vance?" She held the stick above her head, frozen in surprise. Tony turned his flashlight back on.

"What are you doing down here?" they both asked in amazement.

"Well, you weren't around, and Andrea needed to rescue Tony," Sarah replied stiffly, looking uncomfortable.

"You're wearing my clothes," Vance pointed out. "You're pretty good with that stick," he added, new respect in his voice, as he rubbed his head. "I think I'll have a few goose eggs."

"Oh, Vance," Sarah giggled, leaning into him.

Vance's eyes brightened, then his gaze slid past Andrea. Looking embarrassed, he ducked his head, looking so much like Grandpa Talbot that she instantly forgave him for taking off on her like that.

"I'm sorry I left you alone, Andrea. I just got so worried about Beanie. I'm sure glad I came looking for you now."

"Me too," Andrea replied, "even though you're too late. Sarah and I rescued Tony! But they have Beanie hidden in the tunnels somewhere. We need to find her!"

Worry creased Vance's forehead. "She could be anywhere down here."

"Come on," Tony said, dancing his little jig of excitement. "What are we waiting for? Let's go rescue Beanie!" He jumped up and down hard a few times, causing the coins in the bag to clink and rattle. "Hear that? I have Mean-Eyed Max's money! That's what they want. Come on. We can use it to ransom Beanie."

SETTING THE TRAP

Vance thought about it for about thirty seconds as they all whirled around, heading back toward the Forbidden tunnel. Then common sense took over. "I think we'd better just go back to Rosie's for now and make a plan."

Following Vance, they quickly retraced their steps back to the Windy tunnel and up the staircase to the surface. Dawn was just bursting forth as they rushed up Ominica Street toward Rosie's place.

Sitting around the kitchen table eating breakfast, sunshine streaming in through the window, they quickly filled Kami in on all of the events and then talked about how to rescue Beanie. "I'm glad Rosie is at the newspaper office writing her articles. I don't want any adults involved in this," Vance said flatly,

staring at the worried faces around him. They all nodded solemnly, promising not to tell.

"And what do we do about Eddie?" Kami demanded.
"How do we get him out of jail?"

Andrea paused, frowning. "I remember overhearing the police talking about the Chinese workers
being able to pay for their Head Tax. If they had the
money, they were free to go. If not, they were being
detained and then deported."

"How much is the Head Tax right now?" Andrea
asked, remembering that it had reached as high as five
hundred dollars.

"One hundred dollars."

"We'll never be able to come up with that amount
of money," Andrea sighed.

"I don't know about that," Tony said, pulling the
heavy cloth sack out of his backpack and dumping the
contents on the table.

"I've never seen so much money in my life!" Sarah
said.

"That money is why they kidnapped Beanie!"
Vance retorted, angrily snatching the sack out of
Tony's hands and shoving the coins and bills back into
it. "I'm taking it to Mean-Eyed Max now and getting
Beanie back."

"Is that what we should do?" Sarah asked. "Do we
have a guarantee that he'll set her free?"

"He gave his word," Vance retorted, both hands

squeezing the mouth of the bag closed.

Andrea snorted. "I wouldn't trust the word of a gangster like him. Come on, Vance! I know you're worried about Beanie, but don't lose your head on this. Don't do something foolish that may get you both killed." Gently, she pried the bag out of Vance's tense fingers.

Chilled to the bone, Tony leaned closer to Sarah for comfort. "I wish Beanie had never been kidnapped. What if we never see her again?"

"I don't think we should leave all the money in the bag," Andrea said, opening the bag and stirring the coins and bills with her fingers. "If we do, and they get the bag but we don't have Beanie, then what? We won't have anything they want then."

"Well, what should we do then?" Vance asked, irritated. He just wanted Beanie home, safe and sound.

"Let me think for a minute," Andrea murmured, letting the coins slip through her fingers and onto the wooden table.

The heavy sound of footsteps pounded up the stairs. "Who's that?" Kami asked, her eyes huge with fear, as Andrea swept the money back into the bag and shoved it under the table.

"Mean-Eyed Max," Sarah whispered, delicate fingers against her lips. She grabbed the broom from behind the door and stood poised and ready to swing. A polite tapping knock sounded on the closed door.

"Don't open the door," Vance mouthed, shaking his head, wildly waving his arms.

The knock came again, louder and more insistent this time. It sounded like cannon shots in the silent kitchen. Andrea held her breath, praying the person would go away. If it was Mean-Eyed Max or one of his cohorts, they were all in trouble!

They all watched, frozen in fear, as the doorknob turned and the door swung open a crack. "Anybody home?"

"It's Jack," Vance said, relief echoing in the words. "I wonder what he wants." He opened the door.

Jack stood, pale and shaking, on the top step. "Mean-Eyed Max sent me," he said without preamble. "He has a message for you about your sister. He said that if you want to see her alive, you better meet him in Crescent Park and bring his property. And don't tell anyone, not Rosie, not your stepfather, or anyone else, if you want to see your little sister alive..."

Vance paled visibly, looking sick. He nodded. "Beanie's life depends on it."

It was quickly decided that Vance, Andrea, and Tony would carry out Operation Catch Max, as the job was dubbed. Kami couldn't help and was frustrated to be penned up inside when the group needed her.

She was dubbed the babysitter, along with Sarah, but that was to make her feel like she was contributing something to the rescue operation.

Andrea was glad that Rosie hadn't appeared yet. It made everything so much easier, especially since Mean-Eyed Max had been so serious about not telling anyone else. She would have hated lying to Rosie and was glad she didn't have to.

Throughout the day and into the evening, the group planned and schemed and then contacted Mean-Eyed Max through Jack, who had agreed to act as the go-between. As evening shadows began to stretch across the town, a message came back. Vance was to meet Mean-Eyed Max at midnight in Crescent Park where the creek was widest. At that point there were many bushes and rocks to hide behind; Mean-Eyed Max must have felt safest there.

At nine o'clock, when most people were safely at home and heading for bed, they began discreetly heading toward the park. Leaving Rosie's separately, several minutes apart, so as not to draw attention to themselves, they each arrived at Crescent Park alone. Bravely, each slipped down the slope toward the creek, finding a bush or large rock to hide behind.

Andrea chose a spot near the widest point of the creek where two cottonwood trees were struggling to grow. She hunkered down between the trunks of the trees and got comfortable. She knew that once night had fallen the space would be lost in the shadows and she would be well hidden.

Looking around, she noticed a young woman pushing a baby carriage through the park, a big white kerchief around her head and tied under her chin. What was she doing in the park this late? That baby should be in bed by now.

Tony caught Andrea's attention as he came into the park, his cap pulled low over his eyes. He whistled as he ambled along trying to look nonchalant. She shook her head, hoping the bad guys weren't around yet. Anyone would be able to tell that this kid was up to something. He scooted in beside two big rocks on the edge of the creek and sat down. No one would see him there.

Vance arrived last, openly walking through the middle of the park, hoping to draw attention to himself. He arrived at the spot and spoke softly to the bushes and rocks. "Mean-Eyed Max will be coming soon, I hope." He clasped the cloth bag close to his chest, keeping it in plain view.

"I sure hope he brings Beanie with him," Tony spoke from his hiding spot "What if he doesn't?"

"We'll cross that bridge when we come to it," Andrea said, her voice firm. "Let's worry about one thing at a time."

Darkness descended and the park took on an eerie atmosphere. "Is everyone ready?" Vance called softly from a rock across the way. "Remember, let me do the negotiating. I'm the one he asked for, and I have the bag."

"But there isn't much money in it," Tony reminded them, still confused by this tactic. "That's the first thing the bad guys will check, you know. They're not stupid."

"There's a little money it in, on the top. The rest is just cut-up paper. By that time we'll have them, and Beanie will be safe," Vance assured them. "We'll have Beanie and the money."

Andrea prayed he was right. If something went wrong, they'd never see Beanie again.

The wait seemed endless for Andrea. She crouched underneath the trees watching the sky grow dark, feeling her stomach clench and heave with each flash of lightning in the distance. She was so bored she began to count the number of trees nearby. A flash of white caught her eye and she watched the woman with the pram circle the park again. How strange, she thought, to keep a baby up so late. Maybe it was colicky. But she had more important things to worry about. She just hoped the woman was well out of the way when the guys came. When would Mean-Eyed Max get there? She shivered, scared and cold, wondering when the rain would fall.

After what seemed an eternity, Mean-Eyed Max appeared suddenly, silently stepping over the rise.

Tony gasped at his size, exaggerated by the shadows cast by the moon. Cautiously, as if expecting an ambush, he studied the area, oblivious to the approaching storm. Standing on the crest of the creek bank, he waited for something to happen, fully prepared to back away and run if he needed to. Scanning the area and detecting no unusual movement, he came three steps down the slope and waited.

Vance moved out into the open, the wind whipping at his hair and clothes. "I'm here," he called needlessly, for Mean-Eyed Max had seen him the moment he moved.

"Do you have the dough?"

Raising the bag, Vance said, "Here's your bag."

"Put it down on the ground and back away from it," Mean-Eyed Max ordered, gesturing for Vance to move away.

"Let me see my sister first," Vance shouted, remaining where he was, moneybag in hand.

Looking behind him, Mean-Eyed Max waved. Stilts brought a smallish looking figure close to the creek, a bag over its head concealing the identity. "Satisfied?" Mean-Eyed Max called back.

Nodding, Vance did as he was bid, then backed away, leaving a ten-metre gap between himself and the sack of money.

Andrea and Tony exchanged worried glances. "That doesn't look like Beanie," Tony whispered.

BACK IN HOT WATER

Kami sat on a wooden chair in the quiet kitchen, her feet drumming on the floor. She felt like a prisoner. She was a prisoner, just because she was Chinese! She shouldn't have to pay a Head Tax just to walk around in public. How discriminatory that was. It was so unfair. She wanted to be out helping rescue Beanie. She wanted to be at the jail, trying to save Eddie. Instead, she was trapped like a rabbit in a snare.

Footsteps sounded on the stairs and the door opened quietly. "She's in here," Kami heard Rosie say over her shoulder as she ushered a tall man into the room. "I'm sure she'll want to help." The man wore a long trench coat with a derby hat pulled low on his forehead. "Kami, this man is here to see you."

"Me?" Kami felt her heart jump into her throat.

Was he a government official, wanting to deport her for not paying her Head Tax?

The man lifted his head and smiled. "My name is Mr. Wong and I have come to seek your help."

"My help?" Kami questioned. "What can I do?"

"You can help me rescue the workers in the laundry. Miss Rosie filled me in on the details of your escape when I was at the jail to see about getting your brother released. We must move quickly, though. They won't be expecting trouble at night, but I don't know how much time we have."

"I'm ready to go now," Kami said, glad to be of help.

Rosie looked around the deserted kitchen. "Where is everyone?"

Gulping, her loyalties torn, Kami hesitated. She couldn't give the plan away. "Oh – oh," she hedged, "they're all out searching for Tony."

Rosie nodded, turning her thoughts back to the problem at hand. "Why don't you use the tunnel entrance at the back of the house? That would be the safest way. But you'll need to tear down the boards that were put up by the police last year. I don't think it'll take much effort, but you might need some tools."

"We don't need tools," Mr. Wong said confidently. "Where is this tunnel entrance of yours?"

"It's in the cellar entrance, just below here," Rosie said, pointing out the window. "It leads right to the underground storage area. Once you're in the storage area, you'll notice a door at the far end. It's the door into the warehouse."

"More tunnels?" Kami said, shivering slightly. She had hated the darkness and the closed feeling the tunnels gave her. "I guess it's the only way." Her voice trailed off. "Hey! I wonder if Tony left his flashlight?" She sped into the spare bedroom and rustled around. "Here it is!" She returned carrying a bright yellow plastic flashlight. "Now I'm ready."

"What is that?" Mr. Wong asked. "Never mind. You can tell me later. We have no time to lose."

They hurried down the stairs and around to the backyard. Mr. Wong pulled open the heavy door and climbed down the stairs. "It's very dark," he told her. "A lantern would be helpful."

"Oh." Kami pushed the button on top of the flashlight and a bright beam of light hit Mr. Wong in the face. "Sorry," she said, shining the light against the wall.

Mr. Wong stared, surprised. "That's a new flashlight. I've never seen one with such a powerful light. What kind of material is it made out of?" He took the flashlight from her and ran his fingers along the bright yellow case.

"It's called plastic. I don't think it's been invented in your time yet." A look of horror spread over Kami's face. "Oops, I mean –"

Mr. Wong gave her a piercing look. He seemed

about to say something and then changed his mind. "We will free these workers first and then we'll have time to talk. Follow me."

Kami did as instructed. She watched, amazed, as Mr. Wong took a flying leap at the boarded-up doorway. He looked like a martial arts pro, one of those guys she'd seen on TV doing incredible feats. He kicked through the door in record time and then pushed his way through the hole he had made, waving for her to follow him.

The journey through the tunnel was swift and Kami didn't feel frightened at all. She was still surprised at Mr. Wong's strength and agility. They passed the boarded-up tunnel she and Eddie had crawled through when they had first arrived in the past. It seemed like forever since she had seen her grandparents, and suddenly she felt homesick. But before she could dwell on those sad thoughts for long, they reached the underground storage area. "There's the door Rosie was talking about," Kami pointed out, shining the flashlight on the wooden door.

Moving around a few crates and other debris, they reached the door. "Sh-h-h," Mr. Wong said, pressing his ear against the door. "I don't hear anything. If there's any kind of trouble, I want you to come back here and get back to Miss Rosie's as fast as you can. Do you understand?"

Kami nodded, "Yes." She switched off the flashlight.

Silently they entered the warehouse and stood just inside the doorway, listening. Hearing nothing, Kami switched back on the light. "The door is over that way," she said, pointing with the flashlight. "What are you going to do with all these people, anyway?"

"I don't know," Mr. Wong answered. "But we can't leave them down here in these horrible conditions. Something has to be done."

"You're right." Kami stood by the door, the light from the flashlight pooling at her feet. So far, so good, she thought. There were no bad guys in sight.

"Now comes the most difficult part," she said, pointing to the closed door. Already the smell was getting to her; she had almost forgotten about it. "The foreman, Mr. Stanford, has an office just this side of the door. He's usually there, on the platform, looking out at the workers and keeping an eye on them. He's usually alone."

They walked confidently now, knowing that the loud noises would cover them. At the door, Mr. Wong waved her back and slowly opened the door. Kami caught a glimpse of the laundry tubs and shuddered. She had never dreamed that she would willingly enter this place again.

"I see the foreman," Mr. Wong said. "I don't see any other guards. I'll go take care of him. You start rounding up the workers."

"But where will we take them?" Kami asked.

"To my café, for now. At least we can feed them with good food. My wife and Kim have been cooking all day to get ready for this. Now, let's go surprise this Mr. Stanford."

Kami watched in amazement as Mr. Wong walked confidently into the midst of the laundry area. Stanford turned to greet him, his jaw dropping in surprise. He lifted a hand, looking as if he were going to punch Mr. Wong, but he never got the chance. As graceful and poised as a dancer, Mr. Wong dodged Stanford's fist and twirled around; his foot connected with Stanford's jaw, and Stanford was out cold on the floor.

The workers who had witnessed the act cheered and gathered around Mr. Wong, who was talking quickly, his voice excited. Kami hurried into the living area at the far end, waving and gesturing for everyone to follow her. The workers got the message, for they quickly gathered their few personal things and followed Kami. Where was Ming? She should be here.

Worried, Kami searched the crowd of workers. Where could she be? "Ming?" she said, tapping one of the workers on the shoulder. He shook his head slowly, a tragic look on his face. "You mean –" Kami couldn't finish the thought. The image of the white bundle Andrea had tripped over flashed into her mind. Ming was dead. Shock numbed her feelings and she blocked any further thoughts of Ming until later.

"Ready?" Mr. Wong asked Kami over the excited chatter of the jubilant workers.

"Yes," she nodded. She was glad to be helping him rescue her own people, but feeling terribly sad just the same.

Mr. Wong led the workers out of the warehouse and through the wooden door, into the underground storage area. "Turn on your flashlight, Kami," he said as he headed for the Forbidden tunnel. "We're taking these tunnels all the way to the café."

CHAOS IN CRESCENT PARK

Thunder boomed as lightning streaked across the sky and Vance ducked his head. A big storm was almost upon them. He hoped they could get this terrible business done with before it broke. A storm would only add confusion and an extra element of danger, which they didn't need.

Suddenly the person with Mean-Eyed Max flew down the hill, grabbing the moneybag as he ran past. It was Jack! "Sorry, Vance, he made me do it," he said as he brushed by. Easily jumping the creek, he climbed the other side, taking the bag safely out of reach.

"Where's my sister?" Vance roared, tearing up the hill toward Mean-Eyed Max. Beanie was nowhere to be seen. Nothing was going according to plan and it was now time to take action of his own. Laughing madly, Mean-Eyed Max pushed Vance to the ground and began pounding on him.

Realizing something had gone wrong, Tony and Andrea jumped from their hiding places as Jack whizzed by. "She's being held in the tunnels, in a belly tunnel near the Hazelton Hotel," he called as he disappeared into the middle of the park.

Suddenly, a man on a horse raced into the park. "Officer Paterson!" Tony cried, recognizing him instantly, wondering briefly where he had come from. He waved his hands high in the air to get the man's attention. "Over here! Help!"

Hearing the thunder of hooves, Mean-Eyed Max looked up to see the horse bearing down on him. With a yelp of terror, he leapt up and ran.

Officer Paterson raced across the grass in hot pursuit of Mean-Eyed Max. He slid off his horse, knocking the culprit to the ground. They tussled for a moment, then Mean-Eyed Max moaned and lay still, his head rolling back against the ground.

"Vance!" Officer Paterson sprinted across the park to Vance's prone body. He knelt beside him. "Are you all right, son?"

"Hey!" Tony yelled, trying to get the policeman's attention. "Watch out for –" but it was too late. Stilts jumped Officer Paterson from behind, clobbering him on the head with a huge stick. The policeman crumpled in a heap, sliding down the embankment toward the creek as the horse moved away from the noise and confusion.

Mean-Eyed Max lurched to his feet. "You double-crossed me," he cursed, kicking at Vance. "You'll never see your sister again!" He raised his fist, aiming at Vance.

Dodging the blow, Vance jerked away and then rolled down the hill and out of danger. Trying to stumble to his feet, dizzy and a little disoriented from rolling, he watched as Mean-Eyed Max spun around and sprinted for the edge of the park.

"He's getting away!" Andrea yelled, charging after him, but he had outdistanced her. She knew she would never catch him.

And then the woman with the pram came out of nowhere, the baby carriage hurtling toward Mean-Eyed Max. It was moving so fast, Andrea could hear the wheels humming. What was going on? Did that woman know what she was doing?! Going at that speed, the baby would be hurt.

The baby carriage clipped Mean-Eyed Max smartly on the knee and he crumpled to the ground writhing in pain.

"Oh! The poor baby!" Andrea cried, racing toward the carriage. "Is he hurt?" The woman was laughing and cheering and Andrea found that really odd. Who was this strange person?

"Yay!" the woman cheered. "I got him!"

"Give me that baby!" Andrea demanded, whipping the blanket away. This woman wasn't fit to take care of a baby. "But —" she stuttered, for her hand had encountered three heavy rocks in the bottom of the carriage.

"Sarah?" Vance stood open mouthed, staring at the young woman. "Is that you? Where's Alan?"

"At home, of course, sleeping." Sarah smiled sweetly at him.

"So you came to help out?" Vance added, looking surprised and pleased. "You were a regular Calamity Jane, the way you rammed Mean-Eyed Max with that carriage!"

"Well," Sarah said demurely, readjusting the scarf on her head, "I couldn't just stay home and take care of the baby, could I? I had to help too."

"And you did!" Vance cheered, kissing her soundly. Sarah blushed prettily, leaning her head on his shoulder. He hugged her close again. "Now, let's go help my stepdad. How did he get involved in all this, I wonder?"

They hurried over to Officer Paterson, who was now sitting up rubbing his sore head. "I just got home and went to check on Flare, since your mother and I couldn't find you and Beanie. I thought I'd give the horse a little exercise and look for you at the same time. I was coming by the park when I spied Mr.

Maxwell and his gang. I figured he was up to no good, so I followed him."

Officer Paterson struggled to his feet, still holding his head. "Help me get that character under arrest before he manages to run away," he said to Vance. Together they put handcuffs on him. The officer searched Mean-Eyed Max. "What's this?" he asked, holding a black logbook in his hands.

"Nothing," Max sneered. "You can't pin anything on me."

"I don't know," Officer Paterson flipped through the book. "I see names, dates, and large amounts of money listed here. It looks to me like we've found enough information to keep you in jail, at least for a while, until we can do further investigating."

"That could be anything," Max persisted. "It's not evidence."

Taking a peek over Officer Paterson's shoulder, Andrea realized she had seen a paper just like that. "Will this help?" she asked, as she reached into the breast pocket of her overalls. Opening the paper, she handed it to the policeman. "We found this in the warehouse, on the floor."

Officer Paterson took the page, studying it carefully. "It certainly will," he said. "The writing is identical. This connects Mr. Maxwell with..." he studied the paper, "with illegal workers and with selling drugs. I think he'll be in jail for a long time to come."

THE STORM seemed to reach its climax. The wind whipped through the bushes and trees, tearing off leaves and whirling them up into the sky. Thunder crashed, shaking the ground, as lightning flashed and sizzled in the black sky.

Watching all of this unfold, Tony realized that something had to be done, fast. What had Jack yelled as he'd run by? The tunnels! Beanie was in the small belly tunnel near the Hazelton Hotel. He spotted a tall figure running across the street, heading toward the Hotel. It was Stilts, and Tony bet he was heading to Beanie right now! He had to catch him, but how?

All his thoughts pinned on getting to Beanie in time, Tony did the only thing he could do. He ran to the horse and, grabbing it by the reins, led it over to a big rock. Standing on the rock, he stretched one foot up and up until it reached the stirrup. Then, heaving with all his might, he pulled himself up and into the saddle.

Wobbling and unsteady, he clung to the saddle horn with both hands, trying to stay upright on the prancing horse. "Whoa, whoa!" he called, pulling gently on the reins, trying to keep fear out of his voice. He had never ridden a horse! What was he doing?!

He clicked his tongue, instinctively pushing the heels of his shoes into the soft flesh on the horse's belly. "Get up, pony," he said, hanging on to the reins for dear life. "We have to go save Beanie! Go to the Hazelton, horse! Follow that man!"

The horse began to gallop through the park, Tony bouncing up and down, his teeth knocking together every time his bottom hit the saddle.

Noticing what was happening, Andrea took off after Tony. She had a feeling he was going after Beanie alone, and she knew he would need her help.

It was raining now, huge, cold drops of water, stinging as they hit his face. Tony was soaked to the skin within seconds, his thin shirt clinging to him like a second skin. Unclamping one hand, he wiped rain out of his eyes, searching for the hotel. Stilts disappeared along the side and Tony knew he was heading into the side door leading to the spiral staircase. "This way," Tony yelled against the wind, instinctively pulling on the reins to guide the horse. "Good boy!"

The horse turned the corner and galloped down the paved street toward the hotel. "Whoa, boy!" Tony called, pulling back on the reins. As the horse stopped short, Tony slid to the ground, his knees wobbling. Beanie was in the basement of the hotel, he knew it. He had to reach her before the bad guys did! Instinct told him she was near that spiral stairway. He hoped he was right. He only had one shot at rescuing her.

Running his hands along the wet wall, Tony found a crack and then the clasp and pulled with all his might. The door was stuck. What was he to do? He had no time to lose.

Suddenly help was with him, for Mr. Wong came from the shadows and grasped the door, pulling it open. "Go find your friend," he said.

Tony smiled his thanks and scurried inside. "Beanie!" he yelled as loudly as he could. "Beanie! Where are you?"

Slipping and sliding down the spiral staircase on wet shoes, he reached the dirt floor. Mr. Wong was right behind him. "Beanie!"

"Here," the muffled cry came. It was Beanie's voice, all right, but it sounded hollow and very far away.

"Where are you?" he yelled.

"Over here," came the reply. Tony followed the sound, coming to the belly tunnel dug into the dirt wall.

"Beanie?" he called again. His voice died away as he heard running steps coming from the Windy tunnel. "The bad guys are coming!"

Mr. Wong threw off his raincoat, leaving it in a jumble on the tunnel floor. "I will take care of the bad men," he said, raising his hands in a martial arts pose. "You help your friend." He turned to meet them, racing down the tunnel and disappearing from sight.

"I'm in here!" Beanie called. Was there no other way to go? Tony wondered, scanning the area. Would he have to crawl through the belly tunnel? Scuffling sounds came from above. Someone was following him.

"Tony?"

Sagging against the wall in relief, Tony watched as Andrea quickly descended the stairs. "Did you find her?"

"She's in there." Tony pointed to the belly tunnel.

Without conscious thought, Andrea dropped to her knees. "Then let's go rescue her!" Leading the way, she began to crawl through the belly tunnel, a hole less than half the size of a regular tunnel, dug by hand and very dangerous for cave-ins.

It was like crawling through a wormhole, Tony thought, mutely following Andrea's noises. He felt like a mole, blind and alone, scurrying through the damp earth. This was a million times worse than the larger tunnels, and he followed Andrea as closely as possible, hoping that this belly tunnel would end soon, before he panicked and made a fool of himself.

Just when he thought he couldn't handle the close damp earth another second, the tunnel widened and Tony caught up with Andrea as she pushed a steel grate away from the wall. They entered a room lit with one dim lantern, with a dirty blanket in one corner and a bowl of water.

Beside the bowl, her face streaked with dirt, Beanie grinned. "Andrea! Tony!" she called. "About time!"

They grabbed Beanie in a victory dance, squeezing the air out of her lungs. Beanie couldn't hug them back; her wrists and ankles were tied together.

"Come on!" Andrea called urgently, grabbing at Tony's backpack. "You have scissors in here. We need to cut her free."

This they did, wasting no time. "Okay, let's go," Andrea said. Turning to leave, she found a very disgruntled Chubbs blocking their way. Where had he come from? Andrea wondered, and then she spied a door at the other end of the crowded room.

"Let us go," Andrea begged, backing away from the door, her arms outstretched to protect the other two. "Mean-Eyed Max has his money," she said, knowing full well that wasn't true. She was just trying to buy them a few precious seconds of time. "We just want the girl."

"Not a chance," Chubbs stated, standing in front of the escape route. "Not until Mean-Eyed Max gives his okay."

"Please," Andrea begged. A tiny sound came from behind Chubbs and she wondered what it was. Vance's face appeared over Chubbs's shoulder, his hand waving for her to keep talking. "Please," Andrea said again, her brain scrambling for something to say. "She's just a little girl."

"I am not!" Beanie said indignantly.

Andrea watched as Vance's arm raised above Chubbs's

head, a brick in hand. The brick made contact with his skull with a sickening thud and Chubbs crumpled to the floor.

"Come on!" Vance grabbed Andrea and Beanie's arms, pulling them into the belly tunnel. "Mean-Eyed Max and Stilts have been caught. We'll send the police down here to arrest this guy too." This time the trip through the belly tunnel seemed to go much more quickly, now that Beanie was safe. They soon reached the Windy Tunnel and headed toward the spiral staircase which would take them all to the surface.

"And please send someone for the other one," Mr. Wong said, coming up behind them. "I left that tall man unconscious in the tunnel back there."

"Who are you?" Vance and Andrea asked simultaneously.

"This is my friend, Mr. Wong." Tony quickly explained how they had first met. "He came to my rescue a couple of times."

"And you to mine, my brave friend." Mr. Wong bowed. "I am pleased to meet such honourable people as you have proven to be."

They climbed the circular stairs, pushing open the door at the top and stepping into the pouring rain. Officer Paterson came running up and grabbed the reins of his horse. "Beanie!" he called as soon as he spied her. Opening his arms, he scooped her up, holding her close.

"Good job, son," he said, pounding Vance on the back with his other hand. He rubbed his head. "I'll have a goose egg there by morning. I'm sure glad all of you were there to save the day! And Mr. Wong." He smiled, shaking hands with the man. "I should have known you'd be here to help the children, even if I wasn't. You do have a way of turning up just when you're needed most. You and I have been trying to pin these culprits down for a while now. I'm glad we were finally able to do it."

"You have a wonderful family," Mr. Wong smiled. "They are very brave."

Vance smiled, leaning into the policeman's strong shoulder. "Andrea and Tony did their share too, Pa."

Officer Paterson's movements stilled as he searched Vance's face. A bemused smile spread across his face as he pulled Vance into the embrace. "That's the first time you've called me Pa, son." Vance smiled at Andrea and Tony over his shoulder as he clung to his stepfather.

"I don't mean to interrupt this, but we need to get Eddie out of jail," Tony reminded them.

Grimacing, Andrea ground her teeth. In all the excitement she had forgotten all about him. "How are we going to get him out of jail?" she asked forlornly. "We don't have that kind of money."

Tony produced the sack of money from his knap-sack. "I didn't believe that Andrea's plan would work, so I brought this along just in case." He handed it over to Officer Paterson as if he was playing a game of Hot Potato and couldn't wait to get rid of the evidence.

The policeman gingerly took the sack as the others stood silently around him. Moments of tense silence passed as he bounced it in his hand. Andrea could almost see the wheels of his mind turning. It was as if he was weighing the possibilities and considerations of what to do with the money.

Finally Officer Paterson spoke. "Actually, all of this money should go into evidence for the trial, but we do have some in the decoy bag Vance was telling me about. That should probably be enough to convict these men, along with the other evidence you have gathered."

He smiled. "I think, this once, we can put this money to better use. I'm sure we have enough money here to pay Eddie's Head Tax and the others as well, now that Mean-Eyed Max, Stilts, Chubbs, and all his cronies have been arrested. It looks like the elusive opium trail has dried up too, thanks to all of you. Let's go get those people out of jail! Come along, Mr. Wong. We'll need you to help translate for us, and help find these people good jobs and good places to live."

"Very good," Mr. Wong said, rubbing his hands together with delight. "And after that, you are all invited to my café for —" he looked at the sky. "It was to have been dinner, but I think that by the time we are finished, it will be breakfast!"

They all laughed. "What a wonderful idea," Officer Paterson said.

"And I may need to spend all of this money, for there are many others waiting and hoping to pay their Head Tax. They are having a huge celebration in my café right now!"

"The money is yours to help them, Mr. Wong," the policeman said, patting him on the shoulder. "Let's go get the paperwork done so we can eat!"

"Sounds good," Vance said. "But I think I better go find Sarah first. She's probably waiting in the park with one slightly dented baby carriage. I better walk her home. I'll catch up with you at the police station."

"Oh, and who is Sarah?" Officer Paterson asked as Vance strode off.

"You'll see," Andrea answered with a secret smile.

THE CELEBRATION

At last the paperwork was completed, with Mean-Eyed Max and the bad guys in jail and the Chinese workers free. Rosie had shown up as soon as Vance had brought Sarah home to babysit. She was writing furiously in her notebook. She was going to have the best story ever!

Finally Eddie was free to join his friends. "Boy, I thought I'd never get out of there," he said, trying to hug everyone at once. Then he turned and pulled a skinny young man toward the group. "This is my friend Kenny. Where's Kami?"

Hands were shaken as voices quickly explained that Kami was at Rosie's house, since her Head Tax wasn't paid. "You are mistaken," Mr. Wong replied, guiding the Chinese workers out of the police station. "Your friend Kami is a guest in my café, celebrating. She helped to rescue the workers from the illegal laundry."

"Which laundry business is illegal?" Officer Paterson asked.

"The one on the corner of Main and Ominica Street. It was just a cover for the smuggling and exploitation of illegal workers. I have been investigating for some time," Mr. Wong supplied.

"You mean —" a sheepish look passed over the police officer's face. "Do you realize that the police have used that laundry facility since it opened! Another embarrassing moment for the Moose Jaw Police Department!"

Everyone laughed, and Andrea felt relieved. Now she knew for sure that the police were honest. They had been using the laundry for legitimate business, even if they got tricked. Oh well, it did happen, even to the best of people.

"Well, are we going to eat?" Officer Paterson asked, keeping Beanie close to his side.

"Indeed we are," Mr. Wong said, heading off.

What a sight! Officer Paterson and Mr. Wong marched at the head of the procession, followed by Andrea and the gang. Behind them, the Chinese workers hurried along, their eyes squinting against the dawn. They had been underground for so long that their eyes were very sensitive to the light.

Rosie and Vance made a quick detour to Rosie's

place to get Sarah and Baby Alan.

At the café, it looked like a party was already in progress and they all joined in. Kami greeted them, grinning and waving as they came through the door. She stood beside Mrs. Wong, helping serve the wonderful food, assisted by Kim, the teenage boy Tony had met the first time he visited Mr. Wong's house.

"I'm so glad to see you, Eddie," Kami said, racing toward her brother and throwing her arms around him.

"Me too," he said, hugging her back. "I'm so happy to be free."

"Me too," Kami agreed, but her thoughts returned to Ming and tears filled her eyes. "I just wish Ming was here to celebrate too," she said.

"But she is," Mr. Wong said, overhearing the conversation. He spoke a few words to Kim, who disappeared and came back within a few minutes, a delicate young woman leaning on his arm.

"Ming!" Kami wanted to hug her, but her burns were still bad. One side of her face was covered with ugly red scars and puckers and one arm was bandaged. Kami squeezed Ming's hand instead. "I'm so glad to see you! I'm so glad you're alive!"

Kim interpreted for them and they had a wonderful conversation. "I almost wish I could stay in the past, just to stay friends with everyone," Kami sighed. There was something familiar about Ming and Kim, but she couldn't figure out what it was.

"Stay in the past?" Mr. Wong broke into the conversation. "What do you mean?" He looked from the twins to Andrea and Tony and back again, taking note of Tony's backpack as he fingered the fabric. "I knew there was something different about you, especially when I saw Kami's colourful plastic flashlight. Tell me, are you really from the future?"

"Yes," Eddie said. "We are."

"What is it like?" Mr. Wong asked, looking around at his restaurant full of new Canadians. "Do things get better for the workers?"

Eddie knew just what he was asking. "Yes, things get much better. Canada doesn't charge a Head Tax any more. Chinese people can work in any job they like. We have Chinese doctors, lawyers, teachers, musicians..."

"How wonderful," Mr. Wong sighed. "It's good to know that all of our work hasn't been for nothing."

"You've done many good things," Andrea assured him.

"You're a hero," Tony added.

"I'd say we're all heroes," Vance threw in. He glanced over at Sarah. "Especially Calamity Jane, over there! Did you see the way she came barrelling into the fray with that baby carriage!" Everyone laughed as Sarah blushed. "You'll always be my hero, Jane!"

"Jane?" Andrea looked at the way Vance and Sarah were smiling at one another.

"Actually, Jane is my middle name," Sarah told him. "My mother calls me Jane."

Vance put an arm around her shoulders and drew her close. "I like Calamity Jane better," he said, swiping the tip of her nose with his finger. "She was a hero too. Just like you, she was brave."

"Andrea was more than that," Sarah said, dryly, though her eyes danced with laughter. "I'm not sure I want to be compared to her."

"Okay, I'll just call you Jane."

"I kind of like that," Sarah said, as Vance put his arms around her in a familiar way Andrea had witnessed many times over the years.

In a flash of recognition Andrea realized that Sarah/Jane was her grandmother! It all made sense now! Grandpa Vance usually called her Jane! Andrea smiled, seeing them so happy together.

Everything should be feeling better, but Andrea couldn't shake the terrible sense that something abnormal was about to happen. Then it dawned on her. "We need to go, Tony," she whispered, pulling him aside.

"Now?" he questioned. "But things are just getting interesting around here! We can't leave now."

The tunnel to the present was open now, Andrea was sure of it. Her gut instinct told her that the sooner they left, the better. "Say your goodbyes now," she advised the twins and Tony. "We need to leave soon."

"I'll miss you, Andrea," Sarah said, giving her a hug. "I'm so glad we got to be friends."

"Me too," Andrea smiled. "And we will see each other again."

"Will we?" Sarah asked, puzzled.

"Oh, I'm sure we will," Andrea grinned.

"Definitely," Tony added.

"I have my horse story to share," Tony interrupted. "I can't wait to tell it!"

"Come on Tony and Kami," Andrea called, grabbing Eddie by the hand and heading for the door. "It's time to go back to the present!"

"Goodbye," Andrea said, fighting back tears. It was such a melancholy feeling, this leaving. Her emotions were torn. She would miss the young Beanie, Vance, and Sarah terribly, but would be glad to Be back in her own time again. "I wonder how we should get back into the tunnels?"

"I'll show you how to get out," Mr. Wong said. "Just follow me."

Waving goodbye while Rosie, Baby Alan, Beanie, Sarah and Vance, Ming and Kim stood forlornly by, they followed Mr. Wong through the narrow passageway and down a set of steps to a dirt basement. "I found this tunnel entrance by accident one day. I was leaning on the wall and it moved. In you go."

Still waving, the kids hurried into the tunnel. Tony turned on his flashlight to help lead the way. The small tunnel twisted and turned, ending up in the wide tunnel under Main Street. Andrea knew right where they were. "Follow me, quickly!" she called to Tony, Kami, and Eddie.

"Sh-h-h," she warned. "We still need to be quiet, just in case all of the bad guys didn't get arrested." They quickly came to the Forbidden tunnel and filed through, each person deep in his or her own thoughts and memories.

They came out of the Forbidden tunnel and passed by the underground storage area. Already Andrea could feel that familiar force pulling on her limbs. Electricity crackled in the air, which hummed and pulsed with faint colours.

"There's the opening," she cried with delight, making a dive for it. Kami and Eddie followed after her, wriggling through the small hole near the floor. But where was Tony?

Hurrying back, Andrea found Tony kneeling on the ground, his backpack in front of him. "The strap broke," he muttered.

"Don't worry about that now, Tony," Andrea admonished, thrusting the bag through the hole. "We'll fix it when we get back." Tony got down on his hands and knees and crawled through the tiny opening. "Goodbye 1920s," Andrea called softly as she followed him. "I'll miss you."

Kami and Eddie were nowhere to be seen. So,

grabbing hands, Andrea and Tony followed the twins into the force field as the magnetic charges began to vibrate around them. They felt the pull begin to work its magic and smiled. They were going home!

STORIES! I WANT STORIES!

Coming through the opening of the armoire, Andrea dragged herself and Tony into the room. Kami and Eddie had been ahead of them and were already back in the basement room.

"We're back, safe and sound!" Kami shouted, grabbing the other three in a group hug. "Thank you for rescuing us."

Andrea smiled. "Hey! You rescued people too."

"Yeah, you're a hero to all those Chinese workers in the laundry," Tony added.

"It was fun," Kami decided, "but scary too."

"Yeah," Eddie interjected, "I was afraid sometimes. I thought I'd be working in that basement forever. Then when I was arrested, I got really worried!"

They all laughed with relief. "Imagine having to

really live like that." Kami shuddered. "I'm glad we're back in the present."

Exhaustion swept over Andrea's tired limbs and she felt as if she could sleep for a hundred years. They stood back, waiting for the armoire to swing shut, but it didn't. "I don't understand," Andrea said, looking around the room. Everything looked exactly the way they had left it. The twins sat down again in front of the computer screen. The two grandmothers were coming down the stairs, calling their names.

"We've actually come back a few minutes before we left," Andrea marveled. "How bizarre!"

"I know," Tony said. "See? My backpack is good as new and your hair is long again! And our clothes are clean! But why is the armoire still open?"

"I don't know," Andrea replied, her eyebrows drawing together as she studied it.

"Why did we come down here in the first place?" Andrea asked, wracking her brain trying to remember. It seemed like an eternity since they had been in this room.

"We were trying to get them to go upstairs and listen to the stories," Tony reminded her, pointing a finger at the Mark twins.

As if on cue, the two grandmothers popped their snowy heads into the room. "Oh," Grandma Talbot said from the doorway, "I see Andrea and Tony have already invited you to come upstairs for the stories.

Hurry, you don't want to miss any of them." The grandmothers turned back up the stairs.

Kami raised her head, watching the armoire shimmer in the dusky basement room. Gazing at Andrea, she smiled. "I feel like we have stories to share too! Come on, Eddie! Now I understand the stories Grandma and Grandpa told us! They're about our relatives being indentured workers and about Mr. Wong helping all of us."

"Yes," Eddie agreed. "And about the friends we made in olden days Moose Jaw, like Ming and Kim."

"You mean Ming and Kim are –"

"Our grandparents!" Eddie interrupted, laughing happily. The twins hurried upstairs, eager to share their story.

A movement caught Andrea's attention and she watched the armoire slide tightly against the wall, blocking the tunnel entrance. A smile of satisfaction spread across her face as she followed her friends up the stairs and into the living room. She couldn't wait for the stories to begin; there were so many wonderful memories to share.

THE TUNNELS AGAIN?
BACK IN TIME. BACK IN TROUBLE.

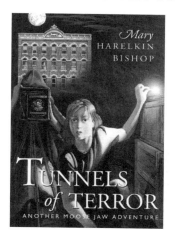

Andrea's not looking for more adventures in Moose Jaw's terrifying tunnels – once was enough! Then her brother Tony lands them back in the tunnels – and back in trouble with a nasty gang of thieves. How can Andrea and Tony catch the thieves? And how will they ever make it back to their own time?

TUNNELS OF TERROR: ANOTHER MOOSE JAW ADVENTURE
Follow Andrea and Tony on their second great escapade deep in the tunnels of 1920s Moose Jaw.

Available from fine bookstores everywhere
TUNNELS OF TERROR — ISBN: 1-55050-193-3

ABOUT THE AUTHOR

MARY HARELKIN BISHOP is a teacher-librarian in the Saskatoon Public School system. Her first book, *Tunnels of Time*, which came out in 2000, is one of the fastest selling juvenile-fiction titles in Coteau's history. Her exciting sequel, *Tunnels of Terror* (2001), was another runaway success. In addition to her fiction writing for children, Mary has published poetry and short fiction in the Courtney Milne book *Prairie Dreams* and in *Green's Magazine*.

Born in Michigan, Mary arrived in Saskatoon in 1970. She lives there with her family.